As Always...
Brooke Baxter

As Always

A Paradise Point Novel

Brooke Baxter

Published by Brooke Baxter, 2023.

AS ALWAYS

First edition. August 20, 2023.

ISBN: 978-0991002238

Written by Brooke Baxter.

Also by Brooke Baxter

A Paradise Point Novel
As Always

Standalone
Christmas Girl
The Santa Scoop

For Mama and "The Legend"

Chapter 1

It was Saturday, and I was late.

Pumping the pedals as fast as my legs could go, I brushed the sweat from my eyes with the back of my hand. The action made my bike wobble slightly to the left, and I corrected quickly. Bad enough I was late, but I didn't want to show up with scraped knees.

The diner came into sight as I rounded the corner, not even checking for cars. I wondered who would be the first to tell Mama that I was, once again, unsafe on my bike. No time to worry about that now. Coming to a skidding stop, I dropped my yellow bike next to the others in front of the diner and rushed in, welcoming the blast of cold air.

There they were—Julie, Derrick, Kevin, Charlie, Brian, and Emily—sitting at our usual table.

Julie looked up at the jingle of the bells over the door and waved to me. Tall and skinny with braces, Julie was the most athletic one in our group and my best friend. She scooted over, making room at our booth. It was the largest one and on a good Saturday, when no one was grounded, it seated the seven of us. Today I was late, but no one was grounded.

"Where were you?" Julie asked.

"Cleaning my damn room. Dad said I couldn't leave until my room was clean." I picked up a sticky menu. This summer, we were trying out cuss words. Our way of rebelling.

Derrick looked up from his menu. "I thought you were cleaning your room yesterday. Isn't that why you had to be home early?" Derrick had a bad case of bed head, with hair sticking up every which way, and his wrinkled T-shirt looked like he grabbed it from the dirty clothes hamper. He was lots of fun to be around, but he was chronically late and disorganized.

"I started to, then I found a book under my bed. I only intended to read a page or two. Before I knew it, it was midnight, and I was tired."

I sighed, still looking at the menu.

"Why the hell are you looking at the menu?" Emily asked, giving a mean look behind her pink glasses.

Emily always wore something pink. She said it was her signature color. We thought that was ridiculous.

"You know you're getting a cinnamon roll and chocolate milk. Same thing every Saturday," she said.

I peered over the menu at Emily. She was bossy, always telling people what to do and thinking she knew everything.

Miss Bessie was unusually cheerful as she smiled and called out greetings to diners at other tables. She approached ours with a swish of her apron. The long, brown polyester skirt she wore stretched tight across her large behind. She owned and ran the diner, as had her father, and knew everyone and told everyone everything she knew. Miss Bessie didn't have any children of her own, which in her estimation made her the perfect parent. She seemed to take pride in telling our parents everything we did wrong. Miss Bessie was our nemesis. But she made the best cinnamon rolls, so we decided the food was worth the betrayal.

"Carrie, isn't that the new bike you got for your birthday? Your parents spent a lot of money and would be disappointed to know you just dropped it like that. There's a bike rack in front of the diner. In fact, all of y'all go put your bikes up properly."

"Yes, ma'am," we grumbled in unison and scooted from the booth.

"Wait a minute. Let me get your order first, although I don't know why I bother. You order the same thing every Saturday. Cinnamon rolls and chocolate milk for everyone, I assume?"

"Yes, ma'am," we said again.

I also wondered why she needed to take our order, when she knew good and well what it would be.

"Well, get on with it. Go pick up those bikes. The front of my diner is not a junk heap."

We filed from the diner into the heat of the morning to untangle our bikes and put them neatly into the bike racks. There were seven of us, and Miss Bessie had spots for eight bikes exactly.

The bells rang over the door as we entered the diner again, and over the din of conversation from the other regulars, we could hear Casey Kasem counting down the American Top 40 from the boombox Miss Bessie kept on the counter. We lived to know which songs made it into the top ten each week.

"Turn it up, Miss Bessie," Charlie yelled. Charlie was the nicest of all of us, but that didn't stop him from being quite the cutup. He was mischievous and funny and probably the favorite friend of everybody.

Miss Bessie smiled and, in a rare act of kindness, turned the dial as she passed the counter. All the diners noticed, and Mr. Carter said, "I wonder what's got into her this morning."

We planned our day over sticky rolls and glasses of chocolate milk. It was summer, and we were free. Well, as free as you could be in Paradise Point.

Paradise Point had quite a history for such a quaint and quirky place. That's how Emily's mama had described it in one of her applications for the historical plaque on the city hall building. Our teachers and some of the old-timers constantly reminded us of its importance to steamboats carrying supplies both pre- and post-Civil War, and of the tragic storms that had nearly destroyed the town during its one-hundred-year history. It ultimately had become a small fishing community on the Florida coast that produced most of the seafood for the surrounding areas. Families had been fishing for generations, and some were still successful. Others not so much. In recent years, it had become a haven for artists and authors, and people who were running away from something. Everyone in Paradise Point had a story.

It wasn't on the way to anywhere. Rather, it was literally at the end of the highway. No one passed through Paradise Point on their way to somewhere else. And no one found it by getting lost on a map. As far as we knew, nothing bad ever happened in Paradise Point, and in the summer in the 1980s, we felt safe. Tucked away and protected from the scary news of the outside world. We had complete freedom to roam and spend our summer days as we wished. I didn't realize it then, but Paradise Point would be the most interesting place I'd ever live.

We were acting up and blowing paper straw covers at each other when we heard laughing coming from the table nearest the newspaper stand by the front door.

"Well, well, what do we have here?" Mr. Lewis snapped the paper to attention in front of him. It was open to the editorial section. The newspaper came out once a week, and Mr. Lewis, the former mayor and a current city councilman, took it upon himself to read the important parts to the diners every Saturday morning, as if they couldn't read it themselves. I once heard Miss Bessie say that Mr. Lewis needed to hear his own voice, because it made him feel important. Paradise Point had as many busybodies as it did anglers and artists.

He cleared his throat, and everyone settled down. Brian, sitting directly across from me, rolled his eyes and made a talking gesture with his hands. Kevin laughed and mimicked Mr. Lewis's self-important grandstanding. They were never serious and were constantly being what our teachers called a "distraction." We laughed at their antics between bites, and Miss Bessie gave us a look. We quieted down because she was sure to tell our mamas everything we did.

"Well, look at this. A new letter to the editor," Mr. Lewis announced. "And I guarantee someone will give that editor a piece of their mind, come Monday!"

He peered around the room, making sure he had everyone's attention. We were quiet, too. This reading differed from his customary Saturday performance. Usually, he read through the highlights of the rest of the paper first.

"To Whom it May Concern," Mr. Lewis read. "Earlier this week, Mrs. Johnson was walking her rather unruly dog, Chester, late in the afternoon. Chester, whom we all know as a menace, took off and ate every bloom in dear Mrs. Stewart's prize-winning flower beds. To add insult to injury, Chester relieved himself, leaving a steaming pile of poop right on her front lawn."

We giggled thinking of Chester, a beautiful golden retriever, taking a huge poop in the grass. Miss Bessie shot us a look, and we regained our senses.

"Evidently, Mrs. Johnson couldn't be bothered to pick up after Chester. We all know Mrs. Stewart is an older widow and cannot afford to replace those flowers. And with her bad back should not have to clean up after Chester, or any other dog. So, in the future, Mrs. Johnson, please be sure to pick up after Chester. If you need bags to clean up after him, you can find them by the community chest in city hall. I have left some for you with your name on them. And to everyone else, clean up after your dogs as well."

Mr. Lewis rapped the paper on his leg and bent over with laughter.

"Who wrote this?" demanded Mr. Johnson, grabbing the paper from Mr. Lewis. He scanned the page, looking for a name.

"There isn't a name. It's signed, 'Just here to make you better,'" he read in a singsong voice, the kind we would use to mock someone.

It was shocking to hear a grown-up use that voice, and it fueled our laughter.

"Don't be such a pig, Kevin. Wipe the sugar off your mouth," Emily said, adding, "Just here to Make You Better."

"Don't be so bossy," Kevin fired back, wiping his sticky face with the back of his dirty hand and grinning. "Just here to Make You Better."

I looked around, wondering who wrote the letter. It had to be a grown-up. We didn't care about things like dog poop, unless we stepped in it. And all of us had picked a flower or two from Mrs. Stewart's yard.

Mr. Johnson was getting his fair share of teasing, too.

"Sounds like you better get that woman in line." Mr. Carter laughed.

"And the dog too," Reverend Smith added, laughing so much that tears streamed down his cheeks.

"I don't think this is funny at all." Mr. Johnson threw some bills on the table. "And none of you would either, if it were you or your wife. I'm going to find out who wrote this and have it retracted immediately!"

"You do that," called Miss Bessie, laughing from behind the counter. "It sounds like a job fitting for the mayor of this fine town. Censor the press—that'll get you re-elected. While you're at it, maybe your wife can head up a beautification program ridding the island of all the waste."

Gales of laughter erupted, pushing poor Mr. Johnson out the door and into the heat of the morning.

Chapter 2

We divided the bill and put our sweaty, grubby money on the table. We always had enough to cover our breakfast and a little left over for Miss Bessie. Our parents made us leave a tip even though we didn't think the service was all that great. It was like paying our tattletale a little extra every Saturday.

The other diners were still chuckling after Mr. Johnson's abrupt departure. We filed out of the diner into the morning sunshine, listening as they offered suggestions about who may have written the letter.

"Probably that upstart editor. She came from that fancy college and has been trying to stir up trouble since she got here. The Becketts already warned her she needs to sell more papers if she wants them to keep paying her," Mr. Carter, the president of Paradise Point's only bank, said.

"Nah, I don't think so. Editors don't write letters to the editor," Mr. Lewis said.

"Besides, the editor has only been here a few months. She's making some changes, but she doesn't know enough people to recognize them outside of their roles in the town meeting. Remember, she got all the teachers confused when she ran that unfortunate story about the science fair," Mr. Lewis continued.

It was true. Ms. Randall, the editor of the *Paradise Point Gazette*, made a mess of the story. Besides mistaking that Mr. and Ms. Lipscomb were married instead of being brother and sister, she implied that the reason Jake Perkins won the fair was because he moved here from another state. She actually wrote that the smartest kids came from out of town. A lot of parents were mad.

On the sidewalk, we took turns pulling our bikes from the rack we had just put them into. Everyone clear, Derrick counted, "Three, two, one, GO!" and we were off. No one bothered to look as we sailed down Main Street toward the park. It was early for the locals to be out, and tourists hadn't yet discovered Paradise Point. We had the streets to ourselves.

Charlie arrived first, as usual, and dropped his bike on the grass by the monkey bars. The city had installed a bike rack here too, but it was over by the bathrooms and trash cans, and that wasn't where we were planning to hang out. Once again, our bikes were in a careless pile. We climbed up to perch on the top of the monkey bar tower. From there, we had a bird's-eye view down Main Street, over the rest of the park and the walking trail, the basketball court, and the marina. It was prime people watching too, and we'd seen plenty from that vantage point. Today it served another purpose: a clubhouse where we could discuss important matters. Namely, who saw Chester poop in Mrs. Stewart's front yard.

"I've seen Chester poop all over town," Emily said. "I'm not sure why someone had to write about it in the paper. Just have enough sense not to step in it."

"Yeah, but it's gross. And, whoever wrote it is right. Mrs. Stewart is too old to go around picking up dog poop and replanting her flower beds," Kevin said.

We nodded. Mrs. Stewart seemed like she had to be at least a hundred years old. But, more likely, she was in her fifties. It was true she had a bad back and limited income, but almost everyone in Paradise Point had a limited income.

"I'd like to see Mrs. Johnson's face when she hears about this," I said. "It serves her right."

Mrs. Johnson acted like being the mayor's wife gave her special permission to tell both kids and grown-ups what they should and shouldn't do. A few weeks before, she had tattled to the librarian that I snuck a Coke into the children's area and was hiding it in the bookshelf, taking secret sips as I read. The librarian kicked me out, and I couldn't check out a book for a week.

"You are the only person who would still, or ever be, mad about being kicked out of the library." Julie swung back and hung upside down from the monkey bars.

"It wasn't just about not getting a book," I said. "Mrs. Wilson also dumped out my Coke!"

We agreed that was especially grievous, but as kids, there wasn't anything we could do except complain to one another from our comfortable perch.

"What if it was Mrs. Stewart?" Charlie asked.

We considered this possibility, but it didn't seem likely.

"No way," Derrick said. "That old lady is too nice. She didn't get mad at me when I accidentally cut her grass so short it died."

We agreed, remembering how much trouble he got in when his parents found out.

"Or remember when we picked all those flowers for crowns for the play?" Emily asked.

"Yeah, she came and watched us and told us how good we did," Julie said.

"No way it was Mrs. Stewart," Kevin said.

We looked toward her house and could just barely see the top of her roof.

"Well, who else could it be, then?" Brian asked.

We were quiet, not knowing who would have noticed and then reported on such a stupid thing.

Kevin finally broke the silence. "I don't know, but I'm getting hot up here and the bars are hurting my ass," he said. "Let's go."

Julie flipped off the bars, landing on her feet. She was the only one who could do this perfectly every time. The rest of us followed and landed every which way. I landed perfectly on my behind.

We dusted ourselves off and untangled our bikes for the second time that morning. Back in a line at the edge of the park, Emily counted down, and we were off. Again, not paying attention to cross traffic, figuring our mamas would be sure to let us know if we barely missed getting killed by a car. Like I mentioned before, someone was always watching and telling on us.

It was nearly noon and hot. We had planned to spend the afternoon at the community pool. There were only two pools in Paradise Point. One at the community center and one at the Johnsons' house. We figured the Johnsons were rich. They had a pool, and new cars, and the biggest TV any of us had ever seen. They were also the first family to have a VCR. We knew this because their son, Bradley, went to school with us. He was weird and always wanted to hang out with us. Once there was an Easter Egg hunt at their house for all the kids in town. We had heard rumors about the pool, TV, and VCR, but that was when we saw it. Imagine a machine that plays movies! It was like having a theater in your own home. It was impressive, but not enough to put up with Bradley and his eccentricities.

The pool had a snack bar, but it was more adventurous to sneak in snacks, even though we brought in the exact snacks they sold. It was one thing to get kicked out of the library for sneaking in a Coke and another to get barred from the only place in town where we could cool off. We decided a quick stop at the Jiffy store was in order to buy our snacks and see if the new video game arrived.

The rush of cold air blasted us as we shoved through the door. Dirt and sweat matted our hair to our faces. We ran to the back of the store to see if *Pac-Man* had come in. For weeks, Ms. Richardson promised it would replace *Space Invaders*. Every Saturday we checked. Today was another disappointment.

Derrick tapped the start button to check the high score. "Yes! Still 87,321! I'm still high score," he yelled.

"Quiet down." Julie pushed him out of the way. "That's only because I didn't have any extra quarters this week. Give me a few days, and my initials will be at the top again."

Julie and Derrick were the best in our group at video games. They were always battling for the high score spot and regularly replaced each other.

"We don't have time for this," I said. "Get your stuff and let's go."

We grabbed drinks and candy and took them to the counter. Ms. Richardson was helping Mrs. Miller, and we stood to the side, listening as they gossiped about the letter in the paper.

"You know that woman won't be able to show her face around town for a month," Mrs. Miller said.

"I know. Can you imagine Miss Priss getting called out for dog poop? Oh, the horror." Ms. Richardson faked a shocked expression, bringing the back of her hand to her forehead.

We couldn't help giggling.

The women laughed, and we tried to stay to ourselves, watching. This wasn't regular gossip and, for once, no one was paying much attention to us.

"I bet it was Claire. You know she's been angry since high school when he took Julia to homecoming instead of her," Ms. Richardson said matter-of-factly.

"Really, you think she's still holding a grudge from twenty years ago? Especially since Bill is fat and bald! Seems she'd be glad she dodged a bullet." Mrs. Miller dabbed the laughter tears from her eyes.

"Yes, but if she had gone to homecoming with Bill, then maybe they'd have gotten married, and Claire would be the First Lady of Paradise Point," Ms. Richardson said in a normal voice.

"But then she'd be the one letting her dog poop in Mrs. Stewart's yard and eat her prize-winning flowers," Mrs. Miller said, and both women dissolved into laughter again.

We looked at each other, eyes wide with delight. This was the best news ever! If every adult in town was busy gossiping about dog poop and unrequited high school crushes, there was no end to what we could get away with.

Mrs. Miller collected her bags and turned to look at us. "Headed to the pool today, kids?"

"Yes, ma'am," we said, hoping that was the end of the conversation.

"Well, have fun, and be careful not to step into any dog poop. I hear Mrs. Johnson and Chester walk through the community center every morning," she said, laughing her head off as she left the store.

The pool was full when we arrived. There were a few mamas there, slathering sunscreen on their kids until they were slippery and pasty white. We didn't have any use for sunscreen and evaded attempts by other mamas to cover us in it.

We spent the rest of the afternoon having rounds of chicken fights, dunking games, breath-holding contests, and Marco Polo. Every once in a while, we'd go to our chairs and eat our contraband. Swimming made us ravenous. It was at these times we heard the grown-ups talk about the letter in the paper. It seemed everyone had a theory of who the mystery author was.

"Couldn't have happened to a more deserving soul," Mrs. Nichols said.

"I bet it was Mary Lou. Remember that big fuss Julia made when her color didn't turn out like the picture she showed her? For months, she was telling anyone who would listen that Mary Lou ruined her hair on purpose and wouldn't fix it," Mrs. Rodgers said.

"Yes, but who could do anything with that hair, anyway? Mary Lou is a beautician, not a magician," Mrs. Atkins said, and the women shook their lounge chairs with laughter.

"But you might have a point. Mary Lou was angry, even though everyone in town knew that Julia was just being vicious. And Mary Lou has her own vindictive streak. Remember when she wore the same dress Claire was wearing to prom after Claire put those rumors out about her senior year?" Mrs. Nichols asked.

The women stopped laughing then, and we moved tighter around our stash of snacks. They didn't know we were listening to their conversation.

"Do grown-ups still worry about what happened when they were kids?" Emily asked, careful not to talk so loud the mamas would hear.

"Only the whiny ones," Derrick answered. "It's stupid. Grown-ups can do whatever they want. They don't have to listen to anyone. I won't care about any of the mean things that happened to me when I am grown. I'll be rich and boss everyone else around!"

We agreed. They were wasting the best thing about being grown-ups. They were free from the past and able to be whoever they wanted.

Chapter 3

Sundays were the worst. Especially in the summer. Paradise Point only had three churches: First Baptist, United Methodist, and St. Paul's Episcopal. I went to First Baptist, a little white chapel that stood on top of a hill at the end of Main Street. Derrick and Emily went there too. We could never sit beside each other on the same pew. We had to sit with our parents. Everyone was sure we'd get into trouble if the three of us sat together. They were probably right.

Derrick was lucky. His mama let him wear shorts. Emily and I had to dress nicely. Wearing a dress wasn't the problem. It was the pantyhose that was a chore. Bad enough we had to sit through Brother Bob's long-winded sermons, but we had to do it in the heat with nylons sticking to our legs. There weren't many buildings with air-conditioning in Paradise Point, and if they had air-conditioning it was too expensive to run it.

Kevin and Julie went with their families to the United Methodist Church. Charlie and Brian went to St. Paul's. Growing up, I thought it was weird that St. Paul owned the Episcopal Church, especially since he was dead. Someone corrected me, embarrassingly, around third grade. But I still thought it was dumb to name a church after a person, unless maybe it was Jesus.

I looked around the congregation, fidgeting and trying to pull the stocking off my legs without tearing them. I'd be in trouble for sure if I ruined another pair of stockings. The choir finished the last song before Brother Bob stood to walk to the pulpit, and there was a bit of commotion in the back. I caught Emily's eye, and she nodded to the side door at the back of the church. Mr. Johnson and Bradley were trying to sneak in between the choir's first and second song after all the forced congregational greetings.

Derrick's family always sat in the back because they couldn't get to church on time, and I caught his eye and giggled when he made a face. His family scooted down to make room for Mr. Johnson and his weird son. I looked up at Mama and whispered, "Where's Mrs. Johnson?"

"Shush! Turn around and stop gawkin' at that poor family," Mama said.

She sounded irritated, but I could tell by her smile she was trying not to laugh. Until that moment, I hadn't wondered what she thought about Mrs. Johnson letting Chester eat the flowers and poop in Mrs. Stewart's yard. Now I was curious. I made a mental note to ask about it later.

I turned around and faced the front, getting in position to count all the right angles in the sanctuary. That was how I got through church every Sunday. Counting the right angles, listing all the colors I could see in the stained glass, or counting the number of ladies with fans. Every Sunday I wondered why, if Jesus loved the little children so much, he made church so boring.

Brother Bob interrupted my counting, clearing his throat, to cover a chuckle, and saying, "Good morning, Bill. I'm glad to see you and Bradley here today."

Everyone who hadn't noticed the interruption before certainly did now, and every head in the sanctuary turned to give the latecomers their attention.

"Well, thank you," Mr. Johnson stammered. Bradley stood there, red-faced, probably wishing he was anywhere but a church.

I felt bad for just a minute and then remembered Mrs. Johnson and the Coke and the library, and I smiled smugly at Bradley and his dad and piously turned to face Brother Bob.

Brother Bob held up his Bible and flipped to the middle. "Today's message comes from Proverbs 18:8. 'The words of a gossip are like choice morsels; they go down to the inmost parts.'"

I looked at Mama. "No story," I whispered.

"Shush," she said, not even looking at me.

I sat back and wondered how he was going to tell us the dangers of Hell without a story as evidence.

"Yesterday, while I was having my weekly coffee, at the preacher table—yes, we know that's what y'all call it—I had the unfortunate experience to hear that someone in our fine town humiliated Julia Johnson."

He hesitated to make eye contact with us. I looked away. I would not let Brother Bob or Jesus ruin what could be the best week ever. And I didn't want to feel guilty about Mrs. Johnson getting embarrassed. She deserved it. And besides, isn't that what Brother Bob was doing right now? I moved my counting to the number of shoes I could see from my spot.

"Now, we don't know who wrote the letter, but everywhere I've been, I've heard theories about who y'all think it was. I certainly hope it wasn't anyone from First Baptist. We know the scriptures, and the Bible tells us it is as damaging to listen and find joy in the misfortune of another as it is to spread gossip."

I wanted to hum so I wouldn't have to listen, but that was sure to get a pinch, so I started sorting the colors of the wood planks on the polished floor. Five scratched planks, four almost black, seven light tan, six with lines, two that had gaps.

It worked. I don't know how long he droned on and on about how Jesus hates a gossip. I wondered if people really cared what Jesus thought, since most of being in church was gossiping about him. Finally, it was time to go, and I was starving. Good thing, too. I was running out of planks to sort from my seat.

After the final hymn, we filed out of the sanctuary, taking time to shake Brother Bob's hand and tell him how well he preached. Even the kids had to take part in this ritual. My parents moved through the line and said what a fine service it was. I said nothing.

I met Emily and Derrick by the climbing tree next to the church. Every Sunday, we played there until our parents quit visiting with everyone and called us to go home. Sunday was family day, and we didn't get to see much of each other during the week. Emily and I had babysitting jobs, Julie worked with her parents at their restaurant, and the boys mowed yards. Sometimes we'd meet at the pool in the late afternoons, but that wasn't always a sure thing.

"I didn't see Mr. Johnson greet Brother Bob," Emily said, settling into the swing hanging from a high branch.

"That's 'cause they snuck out at the offering," Derrick said. "Dad said Mr. Johnson's too cheap to put anything in."

"That's mean," I said. "He was embarrassed. Maybe Brother Bob shouldn't have announced they were sneaking in. Did y'all see how red Bradley's face was?" I asked, a little surprised at the twinge of guilt in my gut for even talking about it with them.

"Well, Mama said it surprised her Mr. Johnson showed up at all. And who cares if Bradley was embarrassed? I'd be too if my mama did something like that." Emily pumped her legs and soared over us so that her pink skirt flew up on her way back down.

We were just about to offer our opinions about the sermon and express our astonishment that people were still talking about all this when our parents called for us. Emily jumped from the swing and ran to her parents, yelling she'd see us later. Derrick and I walked to our families and said bye, making plans to see each other at the diner on Saturday.

Chapter 4

Mr. Johnson didn't need to worry about getting Ms. Randall to change the paper. Mrs. Johnson got to her first.

Wednesday afternoon, I had an appointment for my mid-summer trim. Mama made me keep my hair long, but every six months, she sent me to Miss Mary Lou to take off the split ends. I couldn't understand why I had to keep my hair long. It was always in a ponytail anyway, but Mama insisted.

The Cut Above, Miss Mary Lou's beauty shop, was always loud and in the summer, it was cold too. She had a vending machine and for fifty cents, you got a Coke in a glass bottle. The best part was popping off the metal cap and seeing the cold escape from the top. I wasn't supposed to drink too many Cokes. Something about they ruin your teeth, but I couldn't imagine how something that tasted so good, especially on a hot summer day, could be bad for anything. After a bike ride in the Florida heat and humidity, it was the best way to spend an extra fifty cents.

Miss Mary Lou was finishing up Ms. Randall's hair when I arrived, so I settled in with my Coke and a book in the corner.

"Carrie, I'll be with you in a few minutes. I see you got your Coke there. Don't worry," she winked, "your secret is safe with me."

"Yes, ma'am." I smiled. Miss Mary Lou never told our mamas about the Cokes we drank in her shop. A bookmark held my place, and I opened to the chapter I was reading last. It was the fifth book on our summer reading list. I was usually the only one in our class that made it past the first half of the first book.

Miss Mary Lou differed from Miss Bessie. Miss Mary Lou never bossed us around. They were about the same age, and neither was married. They were friendly toward each other, but not friends. Miss Mary Lou had divorced her husband. She was the only divorced person I knew, and although Brother Bob said it was terrible to be divorced and it made God mad, I couldn't imagine Miss Mary Lou doing anything to make God mad. As far as I knew, she was one of the funniest and nicest people in Paradise Point. She kept our secrets. She let us drink as many Cokes as we wanted in her beauty shop, and more than once she had defended us around town. We told Miss Mary Lou all kinds of things when she was washing and cutting our hair, and she just nodded, encouraging us to go on. She wasn't like the other grown-ups, just waiting to tell on us.

I took a sip and read the first line of the next chapter before I heard something about Chester, and dog poop, and Mrs. Johnson. Pretending to read, I turned my attention to this new round of gossip. Remembering the warning Brother Bob gave about Jesus not liking it, I pushed it out of my mind.

"She came storming into my office, demanding that I issue an apology. Can you believe that?" Ms. Randall asked.

Miss Mary Lou nodded and gave a chuckle.

"I explained the nature of a letter to the editor is for people to air their grievances, and I have no control over what those grievances are," Ms. Randall continued.

We learned about the parts of a newspaper in third grade. I wasn't sure that was the purpose of the letter to the editor, but I couldn't remember exactly. The sweat pooled under my thighs on the plastic chair, and I shifted my weight. I wanted to move closer, but that would draw attention, and I didn't want them to stop talking.

"Do you have any idea who wrote the letter?" Miss Mary Lou asked.

"No. It came in an envelope under the door the previous Saturday morning. It was there when Bradley and I went to deliver the papers," Ms. Randall answered.

"Well, I'm glad someone finally said something. She thinks she can do whatever she wants. Always has."

Miss Mary Lou continued fussing over Ms. Randall's hair, making sure the ends were even and occasionally snipping an errant strand.

"Arlene was in here that week. She complained that when she went out to water her flower beds, she saw Julia and Chester walking past her yard, just as she stepped in poop. Luckily, she had the hose in her hand to wash off her flip-flop. Then she noticed Chester chewed every bloom off her bushes."

"Do you think it was Arlene?" Ms. Randall looked in the mirror at Miss Mary Lou, her big blue eyes round.

"I don't know. She was pretty upset. I've never seen Arlene so worked up. Maybe it's this heat. I asked what she was going to do about it, and she said she wasn't sure, but she was tired of Chester pooping in her yard. She'd already warned Julia to keep him out of her yard and now she was going to take matters into her own hands."

I couldn't believe what I was hearing. *Mrs. Stewart was mad at Mrs. Johnson?* We thought she was the sweetest old lady in town. I couldn't imagine her doing anything to get even. *Wait until I told everyone about this development!*

"I told Arlene I was tired of that dog pooping all over town and had asked Bill to propose an ordinance at the next town meeting that all owners had to clean up after their dogs. He said he'd think about it," Miss Mary Lou said.

Ms. Randall laughed. "I wonder if he'll propose it now."

Our parents all went to the town meeting. It was once a month and sometimes the only thing to do in Paradise Point. Every once in a while, we had to go to the meeting too. They might have us sing carols at Christmas, or give a presentation about something we learned at school. Mostly, though, the kids all played at the park while we listened to our parents argue and complain through the open windows of city hall.

"I told Arlene about my idea, and she offered to second it." Miss Mary Lou turned the chair around so that Ms. Randall faced her. Miss Mary Lou inspected her work before turning Ms. Randall back to face the mirror.

"I told Arlene that if I was her, I'd give Julia a piece of my mind. She lets Chester get away with anything, and Paradise Point has let Julia get away with too much for too long," Miss Mary Lou said.

"You didn't write the letter, did you?" Ms. Randall asked, then coughed as the cloud of Aqua Net settled around her.

"Who has time for that? Besides, I'm not sure it'd do much good. But it's funny. I'm glad someone did. It's all everyone's talking about."

She handed Ms. Randall a mirror and turned her again so that her back faced the mirror on the wall. Ms. Randall peered into the mirror and turned her head slightly from side to side, inspecting Miss Mary Lou's work.

"Well, I hope they keep it up. It's sure selling papers. We didn't have a single copy returned for recycling Monday morning. It was our best-selling paper to date."

"You know, if you need someone to write letters, I hear all kinds of things. You just let me know. There are plenty of complaints to go around." Miss Mary Lou laughed, brushing the loose hair from Ms. Randall's shoulders.

Ms. Randall stood and handed Miss Mary Lou ten dollars.

"You need change?" Miss Mary Lou asked.

"No, the rest is for you."

"Thank you. Don't go looking too hard into who wrote the letter. This town needs a little excitement every now and again." Miss Mary Lou laughed.

"Carrie, it's nice to see you. If this keeps up, I might have to hire extra people to help Bradley deliver the papers. Are you interested?" Ms. Randall asked.

"Yes, ma'am," I said, excited. I'd wanted to be a writer and work at a newspaper since I could remember.

She reached for the door and turned. "I see you writing in your notebook there. You didn't happen to write a letter to the editor, did you?"

"No, ma'am," I said.

Ms. Randall hesitated, like she was going to say something, then decided against it.

"All right, well, I'll see you around, Mary Lou. Bye, Carrie." Ms. Randall walked out into the sunshine.

"Carrie, you're up." Miss Mary Lou swept up the hair on the floor around the chair. A few fluffs floated for a moment before settling back on the heap in the corner.

I walked to the chair as Ms. Randall closed the door behind her. We were alone and for the first time, it occurred to me that Miss Mary Lou listened to other people's secrets, too. And maybe she didn't keep them secrets.

"Cut it short, Miss Mary Lou," I said as she took my Coke and set it on the counter in front of me.

"Carrie, we've been through this. If I cut it short, your mama will be furious. You want to be grounded the rest of the summer?" She wrapped the cape around me and started combing my hair into sections.

"No, ma'am."

"What have y'all have been up to this summer?" Miss Mary Lou asked, focusing her attention on clipping the sections into little twisty buns on my head.

Miss Mary Lou seemed like her old self, and I wanted to ask her who she thought wrote the letter. She didn't tell Ms. Randall, and I thought maybe that meant she did. But I didn't know how to ask her, and I didn't want her to know that I was listening to their conversation.

"Just the usual. Did you know Miss Bessie put in a new bike rack in front of the diner?" I asked.

"Sure did. She said it was to keep a certain group of kids from dropping their bikes in a heap every Saturday."

I looked in the mirror and saw her smiling as she picked up her spray bottle and dampened the section she was ready to cut.

"We got in trouble for not using it. Miss Bessie is so mean."

"Not mean. Particular. She likes things a certain way," Miss Mary Lou said.

I could feel the scissors slicing the ends of my hair. I shivered under the cape. Wet hair made the air-conditioning feel extra cold.

"Well, she thought it was particularly funny when Mr. Lewis read the letter to the editor on Saturday."

Miss Mary Lou's eyes met mine briefly in the mirror. I thought I'd impress her by the way I used the same word she used, but in a different way. If she was, she didn't show it.

"Is that right?" Miss Mary Lou asked.

I studied Miss Mary Lou. Like Miss Bessie, she might know everyone and everything about everyone. She was the only beautician in town. I decided it was worth the risk of getting into trouble.

"Miss Mary Lou, who do you think wrote the letter?"

I watched Miss Mary Lou in the mirror as she gently pushed my head down and trimmed and combed.

Without losing her focus, she said, "Don't you worry about that. It's grown-up business. But it's probably someone who can't stand that woman and her highfalutin' ways!"

Miss Mary Lou was a dead end. That made her suspicious.

She gave me a wink and unsnapped the back of the cape. "You're all done." Miss Mary Lou brushed the hair off my shoulders. "Want me to put it back in a ponytail, or a braid?"

I settled on the braid and when she finished, I handed her the money Mama gave me.

"Thank you, Miss Mary Lou." I peeled my sticky thighs from the plastic chair.

"You're welcome, honey. I'll see you around. It's going to be an exciting summer."

Our group of friends rarely wasted time calling each other. It would be a few years before the seven of us would divide into smaller groups and we'd communicate by phone for hours every day. But I had an idea, and we needed to discuss it.

I raced on my bike to Julie's dad's restaurant. She was taking the trash out back when I dropped my bike, wrinkling my nose.

"It stinks back here," I said.

"I know. What are you doing here?" Julie swung a huge black bag into the dumpster.

"We need to meet tomorrow, the top of the monkey bars. I think I know who wrote the letter. I'll tell Emily and Derrick tonight at church. You tell Charlie."

Julie lived next door to Charlie, and we trusted that he'd tell the other boys.

"Wait!" Julie said. "Who wrote it?"

"I've got to go. See you tomorrow afternoon," I yelled, already on my bike and headed home, my long braid thumping on my back as I flew over bumps that needed fixing. *Maybe someone should write a letter about these streets.*

Chapter 5

Emily was the last to arrive. The rest of us were already sitting in our places perched on top of the monkey bars when we saw her sail down Main Street, yelling, "Wait! Don't start without me!"

She pestered me at church about why we were meeting, but I'd held firm. I'd tell everyone at the same time.

But I wasn't the only one who had a theory.

By everyone's report, all three preachers gave Jesus's opinion about gossiping. We couldn't understand why this was suddenly a problem. Most of them had been in Paradise Point for years. As long as we could remember, there had been plenty of gossip in Paradise Point. Why hadn't they cared about it before now? Maybe it was just written gossip that made Jesus mad.

While Emily scrambled up the tower, Kevin said, "I heard it was Ms. Randall. Trying to sell more papers. My dad said one sure way to sell papers is to find a scandal. This is the biggest scandal in Paradise Point."

"Well, Mrs. Anderson said it was Brother Bob," Emily said. She was the Andersons' babysitter. "I overheard Mrs. Anderson talking on the phone."

"Brother Bob? Preachers don't gossip." Derrick said. "Weren't you listening?"

"Yes, but Mrs. Anderson said that he was upset that Mrs. Johnson voted against making repairs to the parsonage and this was his way of getting back."

"That's crazy," I said. "Besides, I know who it is. And it isn't Brother Bob."

By now Emily settled in, balancing herself on one bar and dangling her feet.

Julie pulled herself back up to sit from hanging on the bars. "Who?" Julie asked. "And what makes you so sure?"

27

I took a breath and pushed my glasses up my sweaty nose, partly for dramatic effect and partly because what I was going to say might change how we felt about someone special to us.

"Miss Mary Lou."

"No way," Emily said. "Why in the world would she do that?"

"Remember the pool? Mrs. Nichols and Mrs. Rodgers and Mrs. Atkins were talking about it? Mrs. Johnson told everyone Miss Mary Lou ruined her hair?"

Everyone nodded.

"Well, they said she was mad. Really mad. And that she had a vindictive streak."

"What's that?" Brian asked.

I rolled my eyes. "If you ever studied your vocabulary words, you'd know. Vindictive means you retaliate in a mean way."

Brian asked, "What does retaliate..."

"Get back at someone," I interrupted, irritated.

"Jeez, Brian, get a damn dictionary," Kevin teased.

"Back to what I was saying. Miss Mary Lou got mad at Mrs. Johnson. She was just waiting for the right opportunity. That opportunity came at Mrs. Stewart's hair appointment last week."

I paused for dramatic effect. Emily waved me on.

"You know how Miss Mary Lou talks to you when she cuts your hair? Well, she was talking to Mrs. Stewart, like always, and Mrs. Stewart told her all about it."

"But how do you know Miss Mary Lou wrote the letter?" Charlie asked.

"Yesterday, I got my hair cut. While I was drinking my Coke and waiting for my turn, Ms. Randall was getting her hair done. They were talking about the letter. Evidently, Mrs. Johnson went to Ms. Randall's office Monday morning mad as hell and wanted Ms. Randall to retract." I turned to look at Brian. "That means take out the article and apologize."

Brian rolled his eyes.

"Ms. Randall wouldn't do it and said Mrs. Stewart stormed out and said Ms. Randall would be sorry. Miss Mary Lou told Ms. Randall all about her visit with Mrs. Stewart. Miss Mary Lou said that Mrs. Stewart wanted to make it a law that everyone had to pick up their dog's poop, but Mr. Johnson didn't do it. And when she heard about what had happened, Miss Mary Lou said she'd give her a piece of her mind. Brian, that means yell at her, or in this case write an embarrassing letter to the editor."

"I'm not an idiot, Four-eyes," Brian said. He'd had enough insults to his intelligence.

"That still doesn't mean she wrote the letter," Julie said.

"Let me finish. Ms. Randall asked her point-blank if she wrote the letter. She didn't say that she didn't write it. Miss Mary Lou said that Paradise Point needed some excitement. And she said that she knows a lot about everyone. She could help Ms. Randall sell more papers."

I sat back, knowing I'd made my case. Surely, it was Miss Mary Lou.

"If it was Miss Mary Lou, she could write something about anyone. She knows as much about people in this town as Miss Bessie. What if she writes something mean about us?" Derrick asked.

"I thought about that. But there isn't anything to write about us. Everyone in town already bosses us around and tells on us. I think we're safe," I said.

"We should tell someone," Emily said.

"No, we shouldn't. Like Miss Mary Lou told me, 'This is grown-up business,'" I said. "I just hope someone wrote a letter for Saturday's paper." I was giddy with the possibility.

"Carrie's right," Kevin said. "As long as they are making fun of Mrs. Johnson, no one is watching me. No one's fussed at me for anything all week!"

"Come to think of it, I haven't been fussed at either," Brian said.

"Oh, so now you're thinking," Charlie teased.

Julie flipped off the monkey bars. "You know what, I haven't gotten in trouble for anything since Saturday either. I agree with Carrie. No one says anything. If the grown-ups care, they'll have to figure it out on their own. Besides, I think they think this is fun."

We agreed and decided it was best to keep this to ourselves. There was no point in revealing the person who wrote the letter and ruining what could be the best summer ever. Besides, we didn't do anything bad enough to write about in the newspaper. And Miss Mary Lou was right. Paradise Point needed a little excitement.

Chapter 6

I was pretty sure I was awake before anyone else in my house. The night before, I finished all my weekend chores. There was no way I was going to miss getting to the diner in case there was another juicy letter. My shorts and T-shirt were fresh from the laundry basket and this morning I had no trouble finding my flip-flops and glasses. Dad was right. If everything was in its place, I wouldn't waste so much time looking for what I needed. I grabbed my book from the bed and threw the covers over the pillow. *Good enough,* I thought, and headed to the front door.

"Carrie," Mama called.

"Yes, ma'am," I asked, itching to get out the door and to the diner.

"Where are you rushin' off to so early? It's barely eight o'clock!"

"The diner. It's Saturday," I answered.

"Isn't it a little early for the diner?" she asked.

I rolled my eyes and immediately wished I hadn't.

"Don't be disrespectful."

Mama caught the eye roll.

"I'm not being disrespectful. You're making me late."

Mama watched me carefully. I tried to look as innocent as possible, but I wanted to get on my bike and get into our booth.

"Okay. Go on. I'll see you this afternoon."

Released, I rushed out the door.

"Don't get into any trouble," Mama called out as the screen door slammed behind me.

I made it to the diner in record time and was the first one in our booth. The other regulars were already there. The preacher table was full, and they were on their second cup of coffee. I could tell because Miss Bessie just left them a pot on the table so they could serve themselves after the first cup.

Mr. Lewis and Mr. Carter were at their table. Mr. Johnson's seat was empty. I wondered if he'd show up today.

The anticipation was electric. Everyone was talking about the letter, and wondered if there would be another one today. Customers who usually avoided the diner on the weekend entered as groups, filling tables, and I hoped my friends would hurry and get here. Otherwise, Miss Bessie might make me move to accommodate other customers.

I feigned interest in the menu to avoid making eye contact with Miss Bessie. After what seemed like forever, the bells over the door announced the rest of the crew. They rushed to the booth with a quick good morning to Miss Bessie.

"Look who's here early," Charlie said with a grin.

"Yeah, and look who barely made it on time," I said. "Where were y'all? I was worried Miss Bessie would make me move!"

"Stop worrying. We're here now," Emily said, reaching for a menu.

We discussed our breakfast options before settling on our usual.

Miss Bessie made her way to our table. "I'll be out with your cinnamon rolls and chocolate milk in a minute," she said, on her way to the kitchen.

"Yes, ma'am," we said.

"Y'all don't dawdle today. It's busier than usual, and I'm gonna need this table."

I wanted to say something about being a paying customer and thought better of it.

"Yes, ma'am," we said.

Once she was out of earshot and talking to the customers at another table, we huddled in tight. There were important things to discuss.

"I didn't see a paper next to Mr. Lewis when we came in," Brian said.

"There aren't any in the rack either." I nodded toward the empty rack by Mr. Lewis's table.

It had never occurred to us to stop at any of the other places in town and buy a paper ourselves. But, I guess, until now, we'd never cared what was in the paper.

Miss Bessie set our chocolate milk and cinnamon rolls on the table, and we wasted no time in grabbing for them, Julie nearly knocking Derrick's glass out of his hand.

"Hey! Watch it," Derrick said.

"Sorry. Move out of my way," Julie mumbled with a mouthful of cinnamon roll.

Emily tossed napkins at both of them and wiped the crumbs from the table. Crisis averted. We ate in silence. The hum of the conversation from the rest of the diners continued until the bells over the door announced another arrival.

Bradley Johnson entered, red-faced and sweaty, carrying a stack of papers.

"Just put them on the rack, Bradley," Miss Bessie said.

"Yes, ma'am." Bradley lifted the wire weight and snapped it down once the stack was in place.

"Thank you. Do you have time for a Coke this morning?" Miss Bessie asked. "It's so hot outside already. I'm sure Carrie and her friends would make room for you at their booth." She looked at us as if to say we better not refuse.

Bradley looked our way. I glanced over at Miss Bessie and then back at Bradley and tried to work up what I thought was a welcoming smile. Emily said I looked constipated.

"No, ma'am. Thank you, but Ms. Randall and I still have papers to deliver. We got a later start than usual this morning."

Bradley glanced at our table once more and waved before walking out of the diner to deliver the rest of the papers.

Mr. Lewis walked to the rack and put his money in the coin box. The wire released, and he lifted it so he could pull out the copy on the top of the stack.

We waited. Too excited to speak. I wondered whether there would be another letter.

From his seat, Mr. Lewis opened the paper and perused each page. The diners hushed as he cleared his throat, and I knew there was another letter.

"Well, look here. This is very interesting news," Mr. Lewis said.

"According to this, the fishing will be best on Sunday off of Palmetto Point. There is a reminder that the deadline to submit concerns to be discussed at the town meeting is this Thursday. You may drop them in the box at city hall. Oh, here, this might interest some of you." He looked over his glasses at the diner, before snapping the paper.

"The Fine Christian Ladies Association will meet next week for their Bible study and coffee at St. Paul's Episcopal. Topic of study is Speaking the Truth in Love."

The diners laughed, and finally Mr. Carter said, "Get to the good stuff. Is there a letter or not?"

"All in good time, good sir," Mr. Lewis said with a twinkle in his eye.

The anticipation in the room was palpable.

"Ah, here it is." Mr. Lewis turned to the last page and folded the paper over so the Letter to the Editor section was at the top.

"To Whom it May Concern. I am pleased to let you know Chester has only pooped in his own yard and has eaten no plants.

"Unfortunately, another matter has come to my attention. We know that A Cut Above is the only place in town to get your hair fixed. Mary Lou takes pride in her shop and the attention to her customers. So, imagine my shock when I noticed several empty boxes of lice-removing shampoo in her outside trash. Maybe, instead of continuing to spread lice all over town, she should have closed and fumigated her beauty shop. So, if you were there Tuesday or Wednesday, and your head itches, you might need to get a special shampoo. If you can find it. Mary Lou may have bought it all."

My hand instinctively went to my head to scratch at the mention of head lice. Emily and Derrick pushed away from me, nearly shoving Charlie off the bench seat.

Mr. Lewis continued reading, "As Always, Here to Make You Better."

I looked around, and everyone was scratching their heads.

"Emily, the Anderson kids had appointments, didn't they?" I asked.

Charlie jumped up from his seat next to Emily and crowded in next to Brian on the other side of the booth.

"Yes, and you were at Miss Mary Lou's too," she said.

This was bad, really bad!

All around the diner, customers were trying to remember the last time they came in contact with Miss Mary Lou or anyone who'd had an appointment recently. Even Miss Bessie was scratching her head.

We didn't wait for the bill, emptying our pockets on the table in a hurry to get our bikes.

The diner was empty in record time and people rushed down the street, scratching their heads, trying to be the first to get to the only grocery store in Paradise Point. The itchy mob moved quickly, past city hall and the Jiffy store, and rounded the corner to get to Mr. Williams's grocery store. Mr. Williams met us at the door.

"What's goin' on?" He nodded at the grown-ups hurrying down the street behind us.

"Miss Mary Lou gave everyone in town head lice." Emily scratched so much that her hair had come free from her ponytail, becoming a frizzy mess.

"They want the lice shampoo we had to use after Julie's slumber party last year," I said.

Mr. Williams shook his head and laughed. "They're going to be disappointed. Someone bought all I had last week. I called, but it will be Monday before I'm restocked. Why don't y'all get your mamas to check to see if you have lice before you scratch your hair out."

The first round of grown-ups demanding lice shampoo arrived as Mr. Williams was trying to shoo us home. We hung around to see what was going to happen.

Mr. Williams raised his hand to quiet the crowd. "Listen, I don't know what's going on here, but I don't open for another thirty minutes."

Mr. Lewis stepped forward with his copy of the *Paradise Point Gazette*. He laughed and, smacking the paper with his left hand, said, "It seems Mary Lou gave the town head lice and everyone is after some of that shampoo."

"What?" Mr. Williams asked.

Mr. Lewis held out the paper.

Mr. Williams took it and read the letter to the editor. Everyone around town knew that Mr. Williams had a crush on Miss Mary Lou. Since her divorce from that weird artist, he had been trying to win her affection. She had so far resisted his attempts.

"Who wrote this?" he asked.

"We don't know. Maybe you. Surely this is where she bought the shampoo," someone in the crowd offered.

"I certainly did not! And whoever did should be ashamed. This could ruin her business. And there she is, a single woman with no husband to take care of her," Mr. Williams said.

Mr. Williams turned red, and his jaw tightened. "I don't have any lice shampoo. You'll have to try home remedies or find it somewhere else. Check back on Monday."

He dismissed the crowd and went inside the store, locking the door behind him.

We raced to the park and took turns checking each other's heads. The nurse regularly did lice checks at school, so we kind of knew what we were doing. We used the pencil I kept in my notebook to section each other's hair and look for what the nurse had shown us on a film strip in science class.

Lice weren't foreign to us. Emily, Julie, and I had them after a slumber party the year before. The boys had to nearly shave their heads, just in case. Unfortunately, it was just before picture day. It didn't matter. No one's mama wanted to endure what ours went through and even then, they didn't let us cut our hair. Boys were lucky.

"You're good," Emily said as she examined the hair around Charlie's ears.

Satisfied that none of us had bugs crawling in our hair, we climbed to the top of the bars to work out who the mystery author was.

"Carrie, you were wrong. It can't be Miss Mary Lou. She wouldn't have written that about herself. Not in a million years," Julie said.

"I know. You think she's read it yet?" I asked.

"Hard to tell. But I bet Mr. Williams will let her know. He seemed pretty pissed off," Kevin said. Kevin lived next door to Miss Mary Lou and told us that Mr. Williams was frequently at Miss Mary Lou's fixing things, or bringing her groceries, and once he even brought her flowers on Valentine's Day. Emily, Julie, and I thought that was sweet. The boys thought it was stupid. Kevin would know soon enough if she found out.

"Okay. Then who could it be?" I asked. "Who hates Mrs. Johnson and Miss Mary Lou so much that they'd embarrass them like that?"

Chapter 7

We didn't have to wait long to find out whether Miss Mary Lou had read the letter to the editor. By the time we got to the pool that afternoon, Mrs. Johnson was old news. All the mamas could talk about was Miss Mary Lou and how itchy their heads were. It turns out even people who had never had head lice have an itchy scalp when they think about it.

Miss Mary Lou had read the paper. Well, she read it after all of her Saturday appointments canceled. We heard Mrs. Rodgers telling another mama about it at the pool.

"I just explained I needed to cancel today. Mary Lou was upset and asked if it had to do with today's As Always letter. She said I was the third cancelation for today." Mrs. Rodgers took a long drink from her iced tea and continued spreading the coconut-scented tanning oil on her already tan legs.

"I feel bad for her. It's her business. And after that awful rumor Julia started, this can't be good. But I don't want my kids getting lice!" She shook her head and reached instinctively to soothe her itchy scalp.

"So, what did you say?" Mrs. Anderson took a long sip from her frosty glass and fanned herself.

"I said I was sorry, but it did, and she was furious! I've never heard such language from a lady."

"Well, someone accused her of spreading head lice, and no one ever said Mary Lou was a lady." Mrs. Anderson chuckled.

I felt bad for Miss Mary Lou.

"Yeah, but it serves her right. She tried to keep it a secret. She has dirt on everyone in Paradise Point. It was a matter of time before someone spilled some of her secrets."

We looked at one another. It didn't occur to us that Miss Mary Lou, the keeper of our secrets, had secrets of her own. Besides, didn't everyone in town already know about her divorce? Brother Bob said that was the worst thing a person could do. *Was spreading lice worse than getting a divorce? What else was Miss Mary Lou hiding?*

"Carrie, you got a haircut last week. Did she seem like she had lice?" Julie asked.

I thought back to my time in Miss Mary Lou's chair.

"No. Everything seemed like normal to me," I said.

"You said Ms. Randall was there, too. Did she seem like she had lice?" Emily asked.

"Nope. Well, at least, she wasn't scratching her head," I answered.

"And you don't have lice. Emily checked," Derrick said.

"What if it isn't true?" Kevin asked. "What if someone just made it up?"

"Then how does that explain why Mr. Williams is out of lice shampoo? He said someone bought all of it," Brian said.

"And the letter said there were empty bottles in her trash. It had to be her," Emily said.

It didn't seem right to me.

"But Miss Mary Lou has her brushes and combs in that blue stuff. And she uses a different one for each person," I said. "If she was spreading head lice to all of her customers, then why didn't I get them?"

The conversation ended. We were at a loss. The person we thought wrote the letter, in this week's paper, certainly didn't. We didn't know where to go in our investigation from here, so we spent the rest of the day swimming until it was time to go home. By the end of the day, with sunburned skin and growling stomachs, we hadn't given Miss Mary Lou or head lice another thought.

Sunday morning was hot and humid. It rained overnight. Even with the windows open, the church felt stuffier than usual. Worse, the cloud of church ladies' perfume hung oppressively around us. I felt a headache coming on.

We took our seats, and I prepared for my familiar counting exercise to ease the interminable boredom of church. The Johnsons filled their regular pew, like nothing had happened. As if the entire town hadn't spent a week gossiping about Chester pooping in Mrs. Stewart's yard. Attention spans in small towns were notoriously short. I guess she felt like the coast was clear since now everyone was talking about Miss Mary Lou and the lice. To be fair, getting lice was worse than stepping in fresh dog poop.

I looked back at Mrs. Johnson and caught Bradley's eye. He gave a quick wave, but Mama made me turn around before I could respond.

There was a loud hiss from the front of the church as the choir sank into their padded chairs. From the pulpit, Brother Bob thanked them for their wonderful offering to the Lord. I thought the Lord wanted money. Isn't that why they had those little envelopes in the back of the pews? If I could just sing for the Lord, then I could keep the offering money Mama gave me every Sunday morning.

I was considering how to spend an extra dollar a week when Brother Bob asked everyone to turn to Psalm 91. Mama opened to the middle of her Bible, and I counted neckties. Three striped, two solid, five patterned, one polka-dotted. Mama nudged me and held out my Bible, the one they gave us in front of the church in second grade. I used the trick I learned in Sunday school. I opened it to the middle and tried to figure out where Brother Bob was reading. After a few lines, I gave up. He was going too fast and I really didn't care anyway. So, I pretended to read while I counted the vowels in the sentences. The congregation interrupted my counting with their snickering and giggles. I caught Brother Bob saying something about pestilence walking around in the dark.

Brother Bob was silent as he searched the eyes facing him. Our pew shook a little with the stifled laughter.

"Mrs. Jackson, is something amusing you that you'd like to share with the rest of us?" Brother Bob asked.

Mrs. Jackson was the church secretary, the president of the Fine Christian Ladies Association, and the most prim and proper lady in Paradise Point. If Emily thought she was the boss of our group, Mrs. Jackson thought she was the boss of the church.

I looked across the aisle at Mrs. Jackson. It looked like she had stuffed a pink lace-trimmed handkerchief in her mouth to disguise her laughter. The entire church looked in her direction, and she fully surrendered to her impulse. Taking her hand away from her face, she let out a loud gale of giggles and leaned over, clutching her side and gasping for air. It was contagious, and the rest of the congregation refused to continue holding it in.

I looked at Emily, and she looked back, wide-eyed. Our parents had escorted us out of church more than once for a severe case of the giggles. We'd rarely seen grown-ups laugh in church except politely at one of Brother Bob's dumb jokes that wasn't hilarious. The only other time grown-ups had laughed like this was when Mr. Belton, who was as old as God and deaf as a post, farted right in the middle of the sermon, unaware that anyone heard or smelled it.

I turned and saw Derrick. He shrugged, and I did the same. The only kid in the church laughing was Bradley. I guess he was glad the focus was finally on someone else, and he was enjoying the show.

Brother Bob tapped his foot and cleared his throat. It was no use. No one could hear him over the laughter. No longer politely stifled giggles, this was full, shoulder-shaking laughing, and it would just have to run its course.

I sat back and waited. Mama and Dad were laughing too. I tried to remember what pestilence was and wondered why that word especially set off the crowd. I wished I was sitting next to Emily and Derrick. No one was watching us now, and we wouldn't get in trouble for passing notes as we tried to figure out what was going on.

Brother Bob waited until the laughing became gasps for air that settled into sighs before continuing. "I see y'all find David's words humorous this morning."

"Surely, this was a prophetic verse, especially since Mary Lou's beauty shop has become a refuge for pestilence," said a voice from the back of the church.

And just like that, the laughter started again, this time accompanied by a fair amount of head scratching.

"That's enough. David wasn't talking about head lice," Brother Bob said. "Besides, we will not bring the gossip of the town into this house of worship."

His hardened jaw and sharp tone sucked the laughing right out of the grown-ups, and they sat straight and still. Brother Bob took a deep breath and started again. I don't remember any of the sermon. But to this day, I can't read Psalm 91 without thinking about head lice and poorly timed farts.

Chapter 8

Since I could remember, the preachers of Paradise Point tried to create unity. They may have differed on things like baptism, drinking, and communion, but they all agreed that Christians, of all types, should fellowship together. Their most successful endeavors were the monthly community potluck picnics and the Fine Christian Ladies Association. Potluck Sundays were our favorite. It meant we could spend Sunday afternoon together, but mostly it meant that we didn't have to dress up for church since we'd be outside most of the day.

The potluck rotated between churches, and once a quarter it was at the park, the place we loved to hang out the most. The park was within walking distance of all the churches, and we often wondered why they didn't just have it there every month. As usual, no one really cared what we thought.

It took some time to help our mamas carry everything to the park after church. Before church, the Fine Christian Ladies Association directed their husbands to set up long tables to display their very best recipes, and to bring down coolers of sweet tea and lemonade. You could tell which husbands had to help with the setup. They were the cranky and sweaty ones during church. Maybe they shouldn't have married such Fine Christian Ladies.

Although the ladies served the food from one central location, everyone was free to sit and mingle with members from the other churches. The grown-ups expected the kids to sit on blankets on the ground. They reserved picnic tables for themselves. That was fine with us. This way, no one paid attention to what we were doing or eating. So, with plates loaded down with dessert and one piece of fried chicken, we grabbed our lemonade and staked out our usual place away from the grown-ups. Here we were, free to discuss our latest theories out of earshot of the grown-ups.

Emily's mama set out an old quilt for us to sit on. Thankfully, each square in the design was a different color: red, yellow, pink, and various shades of blue and green, so we didn't worry too much when we spilled anything. Someone spilled something at every church potluck picnic. Last month, Julie dropped a piece of barbecue chicken on the quilt as she sat down. This time, Derrick's chocolate meringue pie flipped right off his plate as he was getting settled into the spot between Emily and me.

"What the hell, Derrick?" Emily said, as it narrowly missed her knee.

"Sorry," he said, trying to salvage what he could back onto his plate. Licking his fingers on his left hand, he used the napkin Julie offered to wipe the chocolate off the quilt with his right.

"Stop it! You're making the mess worse." Emily pushed him to the side. "Just move. I'll do it."

While the rest of us settled onto the blanket, she blotted up what she could and put a napkin over the spot so no one would sit in it. A welcome breeze blew in from the beach, and we didn't notice until later that the napkin had blown off into the grass.

Everyone in their place, balancing plates on our laps, we brought our theories to the group.

"So, it wasn't Miss Mary Lou," I said, opening the discussion.

"No, and you should have heard what she said about the letter." Kevin took a big bite of banana pudding. "Mr. Williams came by last night. I was in the backyard, and they couldn't see me," he said with a mouthful.

We waited while he swallowed. His bites were so big, it was an absolute wonder he didn't choke to death at every meal.

"Anyway, he came by with the paper, but she'd already seen it. She was working in her garden, mostly yanking weeds from her tomato plants and throwing them in the yard."

"Get to it," Emily said impatiently.

"As I was saying," he swallowed his next bite, "she was cussin' up a storm insisting 'that vile bitch,' Mrs. Johnson, wrote the letter to destroy her business. Then she moved on to Ms. Randall."

"Ms. Randall?" I asked.

"Yeah. She said, 'I offered to help that woman with juicy stories for her paper. What was she thinking? I know all about her little tryst with Joe, and I bet his wife doesn't!' before Mr. Williams told her to keep her voice down. He was afraid someone would hear her."

"I guess he was right," I said. It shocked us that something untoward was going on between Ms. Randall and Mr. Joe, one of the fishing guides in town, but even we knew that kind of gossip was going too far. Especially on Sunday at a church picnic. Jesus would definitely have something to say about gossiping about adultery.

"Yeah, but that wasn't all." Kevin drank the rest of his lemonade, smacking his lips when he finished. "She had something to say about just about every lady in town—Mrs. Anderson, Mrs. Miller, Ms. Richardson, Mrs. Jackson, and even Mrs. Stewart."

"What did Mr. Williams say?" Julie asked.

"Not much. She didn't stay quiet long enough to let him say anything. I haven't seen anyone that mad since Mrs. Jackson caught us getting into the communion crackers and juice after that community wide revival meeting last summer. Well, except Mrs. Jackson didn't cuss so much."

We nodded, remembering how much trouble we got into.

"All he could do was tell her that this will all blow over, just like it did with Mrs. Johnson," Kevin said.

"Okay. But what about the lice shampoo? Mr. Williams said that someone bought it all," Charlie said.

"I don't know," Kevin said.

"I do."

We heard a voice above us and looked to see Bradley. He was facing us, with the sun at his back, so at first it blinded us looking at him.

"Can I sit with y'all?" He held a plate with actual food and no dessert in one hand and his drink in another.

"Sure." I glanced around the group before scooting over and offering a place next to me.

"Thanks," Bradley said, and I took his plate and cup while he sat down.

"You're welcome." I handed his plate to him. We might not normally have the patience to put up with Bradley, but if he had a clue, then we'd make an allowance.

"What do you know about the lice shampoo?" Emily asked.

We waited for him to chew and swallow a bite of fried chicken and wipe the grease from his mouth. I noticed he was the only one of us who wiped their mouth between bites. No wonder parents loved him. He had better manners.

"Miss Mary Lou didn't buy the lice shampoo," he said before taking a long drink of his lemonade.

"Then who did?" Derrick asked.

"Coach Thompson's wife."

She wasn't on the list of ladies that Miss Mary Lou had spouted off in the backyard.

Emily's eyes narrowed as she looked at Bradley. "How do you know?"

"I just do," he said.

We looked at each other.

"Why would Coach Thompson's wife need lice shampoo? They have three boys," I asked.

Everyone knew that when boys got lice, their mamas buzzed their hair. Problem solved.

Bradley looked at the group as he finished the last bite of coleslaw on his plate.

I wondered if we could trust a kid who ate coleslaw. *Gross.*

"Because it wasn't for the boys," he said with a smug smile on his face.

"Then who was it for?" Julie asked.

"Mrs. Thompson," Bradley answered, tossing his wadded-up napkin on his plate.

Wait, grown-ups got head lice too? I looked around the group, and it looked like we were all having the same light bulb moment, realizing anyone with hair was in jeopardy.

"How do you know?" I asked, skeptical that he really knew something this juicy that the grown-ups didn't.

Bradley's face fell.

We would not accept this bit of news without some kind of proof.

"Because I pay attention," he said.

No one likes a know-it-all, and Bradley's use was quickly ending. It incensed us to think he was insinuating we didn't pay attention. In fact, that's all we'd been doing for a week. Paying attention to what the grown-ups thought of each other and their places in the social hierarchy of Paradise Point.

"You know, Bradley, I wouldn't be so smug. Anyone could have a letter written about them in the paper," Emily said with a steely stare. We'd seen that look before and it was terrifying. Emily could be bossy and mean, and every one of us had been on the suffering end of her wrath.

"If Bradley said he knows, then he knows," I said. "But that still doesn't explain who wrote the letter."

We were at a stalemate. Bradley wouldn't or couldn't give us any more information, and we weren't sure who to suspect next.

Charlie was the first to stand up. "Let's go swim at the beach." He walked toward the trash with his plate and cup.

"Bradley, you want to come too?" I asked. It might have sounded like a generous offer to include him, but I really just wanted to see whether I was nice to him, if he'd tell me more of what he knew. I'm not proud of that now, but I was twelve and didn't yet understand how manipulative people could be.

"No, I think his mama's callin' for him," Emily said, just before his mama called for him.

Bradley looked at me and then at Emily. "I guess I'd better go," he said. "See you around."

He stood and yelled, "Coming," and that was when I noticed it. The dark-brown patch on the back of his perfectly pressed khaki shorts.

Before I could call him back to warn him, or do anything, Emily yelled, "Ooh, gross. Bradley, the bathrooms are over there," and pointed to the bathrooms by the bike racks.

I tried to shush her as Bradley turned and looked at us, confused. That was a mistake. His brown behind was at eye level of every kid at the potluck relegated to quilts on the ground, and the swell of laughing and jeering was painful. Even now, it makes me cringe.

Bradley and I made eye contact before he turned around as far as he could and saw a portion of the drying stain on the back of his shorts. In an instant, his expression changed from confusion to humiliation, and then anger. With his head held high, he walked through the crowd to his mother, and I was afraid. Emily was right. Anyone could have a letter written about them, even us.

Chapter 9

The Fine Christian Ladies Association was a monthly meeting for the fine Christian ladies of Paradise Point. It was interesting who was and who was not a part of the organization.

The idea came about at the preacher table at Miss Bessie's diner early on a Saturday morning. Each church had their own women's organization, and the preachers combined them to create just one. The preachers never actually asked any of the fine Christian ladies what they thought before making such a drastic decision. The ladies, being such fine Christians, just went along with it, mostly.

In the summer, Emily and I had to go. Not because we were fine Christian ladies, but because we babysat for some who volunteered our services for childcare for the meeting. They figured we were already babysitting their kids, why not a bunch more? Except they never paid us any more for our increased responsibility. We didn't mind, because it was a chance to hang out together, and most of the kids weren't too bad. And there was always good food.

Each lady brought their most impressive recipe. The Baptist ladies brought crispy fried chicken and loads of rich desserts. The Episcopalian ladies brought fancy platters of fruits and cheese and vegetables, and the Methodist ladies brought casseroles and sides. Today was some kind of special day, so Julie and her mama were bringing in lunch from their restaurant. Julie's mama was not a Fine Christian Lady. I didn't know why she wasn't, but on more than one occasion she said she'd rather act like a fine Christian lady than be called one. That was not a compliment to those other ladies who prided themselves on being fine Christian ladies.

The meetings opened with coffee and Miss Bessie's cinnamon rolls. She wasn't a fine Christian lady either. Then one of the preachers would give a boring talk about one of the virtues of being a fine Christian lady, and they would pray before spending the rest of the morning working on some community project. In the past, they had made quilts for sick people, prayer shawls, organized the food pantry, and put together backpacks and school supplies for children in Paradise Point who needed a little extra help. Then lunch was served, they cleaned up, and they left. There was a system and as long as no one went off the system, things went smoothly.

Today, the system went awry.

I arrived with Mrs. Robins and her three children and went to the fenced-in section they called a nursery. Emily was already there with the Anderson kids. We were mostly there to make sure that no one got hurt and to change the occasional diaper.

The nursery filled as the younger Fine Christian Ladies arrived. There were nearly as many younger ladies as there were older, so by the time the meeting began, we had twelve kids in our charge.

The nursery was in a different space at each church. This meeting was at the Episcopal Church and the nursery was a fenced-off place at the back of the fellowship hall. There wasn't a room for it, so they just put up a little white fence that was supposed to look like a cute little yard and put some toys in it. We were supposed to keep the little kids quiet and distracted while their mamas enjoyed their meeting.

The entrance to the kitchen, also at the back of the hall, was just off our little fenced-in place, and we could hear Julie and her mama putting the finishing touches on the meal. We rarely liked it when the meetings were at the Episcopal Church because we also had to keep all the little kids quiet so they wouldn't interrupt the Fine Christian Ladies. But we also had to make enough noise that the real little kids wouldn't hear their mama's voices and start crying. It was a precarious balance.

Today, the little kids were easier to manage than usual. Everyone was content with their toys when I heard Reverend Allen clear his throat and the ladies stopped their good morning greetings.

"Good morning," he said.

"Good morning," the ladies returned in unison.

"It is such a joy to spend this beautiful morning with so many of Paradise Point's finest Christian ladies."

There was a rustle, and we heard him say, "How do you handle conflict? We may need to confront a family member or a good friend. It might be necessary to remind someone that their commitment to their faith means they should not say or do certain things. Or we may have to take a stand to hold someone accountable for their actions."

"Like Julia letting Chester poop all over town," Mrs. Anderson said, and there was a twitter of laughter from the ladies.

"Or Mary Lou spreading around head lice," Ms. Richardson said.

Even though no one in Paradise Point ever said they got lice that week.

"Let's not forget, Ms. Randall putting all this in that dreadful paper of hers, trying to ruin our town while she sells papers," Mrs. Jackson said.

Reverend Allen cleared his throat again. "I am so glad you brought this up. In Ephesians, Paul is addressing the unity of the church. Y'all attend different churches, but you all profess to be Christians. Ephesians chapter four verse fifteen reminds us when we speak the truth in love, we are growing more like Christ while we help each other do the same. But we must practice, and how better can we do that than by taking a few minutes to address what has been happening right here in Paradise Point?"

He waited for a minute, and I just barely caught little Joel Anderson as he almost wiggled his way out of the fence and into the meeting. He gave a little squeal and tried to pull away, but I had his shirt and was not letting go.

"Come here," I whispered and picked up the red car he'd dropped earlier.

His eyes widened and his sticky hands reached out to take it, saying, "Vroom, vroom," before dropping to the floor.

I sat as a guard near the gate to avert any other escape attempts. Emily was busy changing a diaper with one hand—the other trying unsuccessfully to keep the stench of baby poop from her nose. *How could something so cute make something so disgusting?* I was glad I was nearest to the gate. It meant I could hear what the ladies were saying. I had rarely cared before, but these weren't usual times.

Reverend Allen took out his Bible and opened it to the back. "Scripture reminds us that when we need to speak up, to right a wrong, or admonish a fellow Christian, we are to do it with love. Not malice. We need to acknowledge that we all do things that fall short of who we should be, but that we are all working to grow in our faith. When these opportunities arise, it's best to imagine the person as Christ sees them and to talk to them in the examples of how Christ addressed people."

I thought maybe even Christ would have trouble with some people in Paradise Point.

"Pay attention to your motives. Are you trying to make yourself look better? Then keep quiet. Will you turn around and gossip about the situation? Then keep quiet. Will this puff you up so that pride becomes a source of sin in your own life? Then you aren't ready. Speaking the truth in love is difficult, but it keeps relationships intact and reflects God's love to that person and to others who may be affected."

Reverend Allen looked around at the ladies, who stared blankly back. I didn't think they really cared that much about what Paul or Jesus said about these things.

"I am going to turn the meeting over to Mrs. Jackson now. Y'all have a lovely morning, and it smells like a delicious meal." He walked through the fellowship hall and gave a nod and a smile toward me and Emily as he passed us.

Mrs. Jackson stood at the front of the room and thanked Reverend Allen, wishing him a pleasant rest of the day.

Once he was out of earshot, Mrs. Jackson took control of the meeting. "Before we pray, let's take a few moments to acknowledge any prayer requests."

She opened a little yellow notebook and unclipped a red pen from the cover. The sunlight streamed in from the windows, bathing her in a rainbow of colors. For a moment, she looked angelic.

This was one time the ladies were not quiet. Rapid-fire, they asked for prayer for so-and-so's marriage because someone had heard their husband had a wandering eye. They asked for prayer for so-and-so's husband's drinking problem. They asked for prayer for so-and-so's finances, because they had heard the bank wouldn't give them a loan.

Emily and I looked at each other with raised eyebrows as Mrs. Jackson smiled at each request, diligently writing the request in her notebook. Since we only babysat the kids in the summer and were usually in a room away from the ladies when we did, it shocked us to see they were being so mean to each other while they were supposed to be praying!

With each request, there were plenty of hushed, "Well, bless her heart," to go around. It wasn't until much later I realized they didn't really mean to bless anyone's heart.

Julie's mama came out of the kitchen and stood next to our fenced area, shaking her head. Julie let herself in the gate and sat next to me and Emily.

"Mama can't stand most of these ladies," she whispered.

I looked at Julie's mama, and she smiled at me.

"Don't pay any attention to these mean old biddies," she whispered. "Well, except your own mamas." She winked.

I searched the ladies for our mamas. They weren't offering any requests, but they weren't defending anyone either.

Convinced she had recorded all the sins of Paradise Point in her yellow notebook, Mrs. Jackson directed the ladies to bow their heads. She prayed with the passion of a televangelist.

"Heavenly Father, Lord, thank you for this beautiful day. Thank you for these ladies who've come together to learn about you and to ask for your guidance as we speak the truth in love. Thank you for Reverend Allen's reminder to look for examples in the Bible of what sins we should identify and correct in others."

We didn't bow our heads, because we weren't Fine Christian Ladies. I looked at Julie's mom, and she smiled, shrugged, and mouthed, "See?" I nodded. Even I knew that wasn't what Reverend Allen had said.

"Please help the Ericson's marriage. Maybe inspire Loretta to fix herself up so Elmer won't stray and sin against you. And, Lord, please help her improve her cooking. Please help the Bakers remember that drunkenness is a sin, and those who cannot control their liquor will not inherit the Kingdom of God."

My face grew red and warm. I couldn't tell if I was embarrassed, worried, or angry.

"Please help the Simpsons with their finances. If they only tithed consistently, then they wouldn't need a loan because God loves a cheerful giver and meets all our needs."

Some ladies nodded slightly with their heads bowed and eyes closed, murmuring the occasional amen. The prayer went on for what seemed like forever in this pattern before she closed with, "Thank you, Lord, for always meeting us here to make our nearly perfect corner of the world even better."

My eyes locked on Emily.

"I know," she mouthed, eyes wide, with a grin on her face. Before we could say anything, Mrs. Jackson motioned for Julie and her mama to serve lunch. The two set plates and drinks in front of everyone. It smelled delicious: fried fish, hush puppies, potato salad, green beans dripping in bacon grease, and puffy yeast rolls. They came around with pitchers of sweet tea, and the ladies thanked them as they enthusiastically dove into their plates.

"Jo Ellen, why don't you join our group?" Mrs. Jackson asked when Julie's mama set a bowl of lemon wedges on the table in between Mrs. Jackson and Mrs. Anderson.

"I like to keep my gossipy thoughts just between me and Jesus. It's much more discreet that way," Julie's mama answered and continued moving down the table, putting out lemons.

"What do you mean?" Mrs. Jackson narrowed her gaze.

I was making plates of peanut butter and jelly sandwiches for the little kids and had a front-row seat for this exchange.

"I'd rather act like a fine Christian lady than be called one." Julie's mama smiled. "And you can write that down in your little gossip book, there. But be careful. You know about living in glass houses and all that? Don't you?"

Mrs. Jackson's hand flew to her chest, and she clutched the pearls around her neck. "I don't know what you're referring to, Jo Ellen. We're taking these prayer requests to the Lord for him to sort out as scripture tells us to do."

"Yeah, well, remember scripture also says that pride cometh before the fall."

"Well, I never! And to think that we eat in your husband's restaurant every Sunday after church. I think this week we'll take our business elsewhere," Mrs. Jackson said.

"Doesn't scripture say something about keeping the Sabbath? Maybe you should cook at home, or is your cooking as bad as Loretta's?" Julie's mama smiled and held her head high as she walked through the ladies. Some, including our own mamas, were smiling. Finally, someone had spoken the truth in love to the biggest gossip in town. Others looked on in dismay. But no one except Emily and me seemed to catch that Mrs. Jackson had ended her prayer with a suspiciously familiar phrase. Now I knew for sure who had written the letters.

I sat next to Emily with two plates of peanut butter and jelly sandwiches. Julie joined us for lunch. Before we took a bite, we looked at each other and under her breath, Julie said, "It's got to be Mrs. Jackson."

Chapter 10

Once again, I was up early and off to the diner. Mama and Dad just looked up from their coffee and told me to "be good" before I slammed the screen door and ran to my bike.

I raced down Cedar Lane and narrowly missed running into a jogger. Swerving, I hit a pothole and would have wrecked my bike had I not caught myself by planting a foot squarely on the ground.

"Hey, you okay?" the jogger asked.

"Yes, sir," I said.

The jogger looked familiar, but Paradise Point had lots of people who'd come and go. He wasn't from here. Sometimes people came to work awhile on a shrimp boat, or write a book, or maybe stay for a season making art. I assumed he was one of those. We called them outsiders.

"Be careful. These streets are terrible," he said and started jogging toward the diner.

I took off again, passing him on the other side of the street this time. Emily met me as I turned onto Main Street, and we rode the rest of the way to the diner, guessing what the next letter might be about. Emily thought it might be about the Bakers' drinking, but I thought Mr. Ericson's wandering eye was juicier.

Diners filled every seat, so we weren't able to get to our usual big booth. Instead, we had to all squish into a booth meant for four adults. Fortunately, we were all still small enough to squeeze in tight. Being left-handed, I sat on the outside so I wouldn't bump into the person next to me with my elbow as we ate.

"Sorry, I couldn't save the big booth for you this morning." Miss Bessie swished up to the table to take our order. "This letter thing has everyone coming to the diner on Saturdays. Chuck's enjoying his weekly performance so much, I wonder if he wrote the letters." She glanced his way, and people were crowding around his table as if he were a celebrity.

"Brian, maybe you should get his autograph," I teased.

Brian carried this notebook with him everywhere he went. He was obsessed with movie stars and sports heroes and wanted to make sure if he ever ran into one, he'd get their autograph. So far, the notebook was empty. It would be a long time before any celebrities discovered Paradise Point.

"Whatever." Brian patted his pocket to make sure the blue spiral was still in its place.

"Saturday morning usual?" Miss Bessie asked.

"Yes, ma'am," we said.

She left to put in our order, and Emily caught the boys up, explaining who we thought it was and why. Their mamas were all part of the Fine Christian Ladies, but they didn't know what went on at the meetings.

"That's just mean," Charlie said.

"It sounds like any of them could have written the letters, as much as they like to gossip," Kevin said.

"I know," Julie said. "Well, except your mamas. They weren't saying bad things about other people," she quickly added, since our mamas were part of the meetings.

"Why isn't your mama in that group?" Emily asked. I'd wondered that too, but only Emily was rude enough to ask.

"Mrs. Jackson did something mean to my mama a long time ago. I don't know what because she won't tell me, but now she wouldn't be caught dead at one of those meetings unless she has to for the restaurant," Julie said.

"Y'all should have seen Ms. Jo Ellen take down perfect Mrs. Jackson," Emily said.

Miss Bessie placed the tray of chocolate milk and cinnamon rolls on our table, and we each took ours, careful this time not to bump into each other.

The diner was louder than usual. Mr. Lewis had a copy of the paper and was visiting leisurely with Mr. Carter and Mr. Johnson. Now that the heat was off his family, Mr. Johnson could celebrate the misfortune of others.

We could hear other people wondering if there was going to be a new letter, and if so, who would be the unlucky person? One table was placing bets. I thought they better be quiet, or someone might put that in a letter. We all knew what happened to poor Mr. Bishop. He lost everything to gambling and had to live in a shack on the beach after his wife and kids left him. His was a cautionary tale.

We waited for what seemed like forever before Mr. Lewis opened the paper with a flourish, announcing that this week's edition seemed thicker than before. The conversations settled down until all we heard was the humming of the air conditioner and the ice dropping into the bottom of the machine with a startling crash.

"Okay, let's see what we have today. The town meeting will be Thursday. It will start earlier than usual because there were so many concerns dropped in the box," Mr. Lewis read and looked at Mr. Johnson over the top of the paper.

"Yes, everyone has something they want to say this month," Mr. Johnson said. "I encourage all of y'all to come and have your voice heard."

"Fishing will be best beyond the South Beach Channel on Tuesday morning early. Most fisherman have been catching their limit every day off the main pier.

"The girls' summer softball team is undefeated and will play next Friday night. I know we all watch, but they still ask us to come out and support our girls," Mr. Lewis said.

"Okay, here we are." Mr. Lewis took a moment to fold the paper over, but this time didn't fold the top over. "It seems we have some furious residents. Dare I say that Paradise Point isn't a paradise for everyone?"

He looked around the room. Excitement was building, and I strained against the table, willing him to get on with it.

"To Whom it May Concern, you need to better vet the letters that come to the editor. I want to live in a peaceful community. This newspaper has become a rumor-mongering rag. Now Mrs. Johnson can't even look at Mrs. Stewart. I saw them avoiding each other in the grocery store. It is uncomfortable for everyone. Stop this nonsense now." Mr. Lewis paused and took a long drink of his coffee.

"Dear Editor, I am appalled at the gall of some of our citizens. Mary Lou did NOT spread head lice around town. I have taken it upon myself and asked around, and no one knows anyone who had lice last week. And why the hell is anyone digging through other people's trash? Whoever this is needs to stop."

Mr. Lewis folded the page and peered at the diners over his glasses. "There's another one. Should I go on?"

There was a resounding "Yes!"

"All right then. Dear Editor, I hope you never stop printing these letters. Nothing exciting happens in Paradise Point and this is pure entertainment. Keep up the good work."

"Well, at least someone's happy." Mr. Lewis chuckled.

We laughed because even though we didn't want an As Always letter written about us, it was exciting to figure out the mystery. I guess everyone in town felt the same.

"All right. Here's the letter we've all been waiting for."

Mr. Lewis's eyes got big, and he hesitated before looking over at the preacher table. "Ummm, this one's a little different. I'm not so sure we should read it out loud."

"Oh, go on. How bad can it be? Can't be any worse than Mary Lou contaminating the town with head lice," one diner said.

It intrigued us. As much as Mr. Lewis liked the drama and an audience, something must be different if he was hesitating.

Miss Bessie looked in our direction and swished her way over to Mr. Lewis, holding her hand out for the paper. He handed it over, and she read it before handing it back.

"Go ahead. Read it," she said.

"Okay. Bessie gave the go-ahead." Mr. Lewis took the paper back.

"To Whom It May Concern: Mrs. Jackson is, in fact, the most considerate woman in all of Paradise Point. Losing her husband so suddenly must have been hard and yet she perseveres, taking care of her friends. We should all offer prayers of thanksgiving that she has time on her hands to be helpful to others. Just this week I saw her bringing pies and casseroles to Mr. Bennet's house, often lingering on the porch for a glass of sweet tea or staying for dinner. It is nice to see a Fine Christian Lady taking such good care of him in his wife's absence. But maybe she should use a bit more discretion. Wouldn't want people to get the wrong idea. As Always, Here to Make You Better."

It obviously wasn't Mrs. Jackson.

The collective sigh sucked the air right out of the room, before we heard some ladies at the table behind us laugh.

"I thought she was pretty dressed up for a random afternoon when I went by the other day. She practically pushed me off her porch," said a woman at the table across from us.

"Fine Christian Lady, my ass," I heard another lady say, and the diner erupted into laughter.

Miss Bessie came by and told us to go on. This wasn't appropriate for us to be listening to, but she chuckled as she picked up our plates. "Couldn't have happened to a finer Christian lady."

It was a rare rainy day, so we ducked into the library to wait out the summer storm. Luckily, the library was right next to the diner, so we left our bikes and ran, trying not to get soaked.

We shivered, arranging ourselves in a close circle in the children's area on the brightly colored carpet, unconcerned that our wet clothes would drip and leave the carpet a soggy mess. The librarian wasn't as strict about silence in that corner, but we still whispered, out of habit. She'd fussed at us more than once before.

"That's just gross!" Kevin announced. "They're old!"

We giggled, trying to keep quiet, which, like in church, made it worse.

"I know. Can you imagine them kissing?" Julie made a gagging sound.

"Why is Mrs. Jackson crushing on Mr. Bennet? He's married," Brian asked.

"Do we really need to explain this to you, Brian? That's the point of the letter. No one should crush on old married people. It's unnatural," I said.

"It's kind of mean," Julie said. "But she didn't have any trouble discussing everyone else's lives." Her eyes lit up. "I can't wait to tell Mama about this."

"Paradise Point is so small, I'm sure she'll know about it by lunchtime," I said.

"So, pretty sure Mrs. Jackson didn't write the letter," Charlie said.

"Nope, at least not this one," Julie agreed.

"What if there is more than one author? There were other letters to the editor in today's paper," I said.

"But only one signed, *As Always, Here to Make You Better*," Brian said.

"We thought for sure it was Mrs. Jackson because she said 'as always' in her prayer," Emily explained.

"Maybe she liked the letters as much as the rest of us and added it into her prayer? You know, trying to be clever?" I asked.

"The letters all sound like one person wrote them," Julie said.

"Okay, then. Y'all said she was really mean at the Fine Christian Ladies meeting. What exactly did she say?" Charlie asked.

Emily, Julie, and I recounted all the *prayer requests* that were written in her yellow notebook. There was no shortage of people who might be upset with Mrs. Jackson. In all of our discussion, we didn't think about how this might affect Mr. and Mrs. Bennet. We were twelve and didn't yet understand how complicated and fragile adult relationships were.

"Okay, so it could have been Mrs. Ericson, mad about her husband and cooking being talked about," Charlie said.

"Or, Mrs. Baker, upset that Mrs. Jackson mentioned their drinking," Kevin said.

"Or, Mrs. Simpson. She's probably upset to hear people talking about them not having money. What's tithing, anyway?" Brian asked.

"It's when your parents give a check to the church," I said. "But how would Mrs. Jackson know they aren't tithing?"

"Because Mrs. Jackson is the one who counts the money and takes it to the bank," Derrick said. "My dad said that old woman knows how much money everyone *does* and *doesn't* give to the church. That's why she thinks she's in charge."

We sat quietly, considering this development as the air conditioner whirred in the background. I felt a little bad for Mrs. Jackson. *What if it wasn't what it looked like?* People around town had accused us of all kinds of things before.

"What do you think Mrs. Jackson's gonna do?" I asked.

"I don't know, but I'm not missing church tomorrow," Emily said, getting to her feet. "That's for sure."

Chapter 11

The rain that started Saturday morning didn't let up until late into the night. Sunday dawned sunny and humid. It was a new day as the consequences of Saturday's As Always letter settled on Paradise Point.

We were sitting in our usual pew when Brother Bob took the pulpit. It was hot, and I kept adjusting myself, trying to find a comfortable position on the hard wooden pew.

I was deep into my counting. Today it was colors from the stained glass showing on the wood floor when Brother Bob welcomed us to worship. Three yellow, two green, six blue, four orange. I strained to look behind me, and Mama nudged me to be still. She mouthed, "Sit still." I settled in and tried to list all the things I could see without moving my head. She could make me sit still, but she couldn't make me pay attention. *God, please stop making church so boring*, I prayed.

Brother Bob took out a white handkerchief and dabbed his forehead. It usually took a few minutes of yelling about God and Jesus and Hell before he was red-faced and sweating, but all he'd done so far was say "Good morning." I mentally added handkerchief, sweat, bald head, red face, gray suit, wood steps, and yellow choir robes to my straight-ahead staring list.

Brother Bob hesitated, his eyes resting with compassion on one person in particular in the congregation. The urge to disobey Mama was too intense. I turned my head and followed his gaze. Mrs. Jackson sat with her head held high, looking straight ahead at Brother Bob as if no one else were in church.

Mama nudged me, and I turned around, facing Brother Bob again. Mama never turned her head. She wasn't interested in town gossip like I was.

Brother Bob nodded toward Mrs. Jackson and, giving a weak smile, opened his Bible. He glanced toward Mrs. Jackson again and took a breath before speaking.

"As I was praying and considering the text for today, I thought of the unfortunate events happening in our community. No doubt all of you know that someone has been using the vital Letter to the Editor section of our newspaper to air their grievances. I prayed and asked the Lord to give me a text, and after study and prayer, He led me to John, chapter eight."

Brother Bob wiped his face again, and I wondered if he would need to wring out his handkerchief before the sermon was over.

"Since you're so well versed in the scriptures, you will, I'm sure, recognize this as the story of the woman caught in adultery."

Nervous snickering went up from the congregation. Brother Bob cleared his throat. Silence settled except for the flapping of fans some ladies used to escape the oppressive Florida heat.

"I spent all week studying and preparing for my sermon, trusting the Lord will give me the right thing to say," Brother Bob explained.

"Maybe he should have led you to 1 Timothy, about how widows should act," Mrs. Bennet said from the choir loft.

Mama gasped that time, and my head almost spun right off my neck as I looked from Mrs. Bennet to Mrs. Jackson, who had her pink handkerchief pressed to her mouth.

"Barbara, that will do," Brother Bob said.

Since Mama seemed to have lost interest in whether I was paying attention, I turned and looked at Emily. Her eyes were so wide they took up her entire face. We had heard women say catty things in the Fine Christian Ladies meetings, but rarely did a woman speak in church, and never like this. I tried to tuck myself in close to Mama, sure that God would smite us all any minute.

The commotion in the choir loft pulled my attention forward again. Mrs. Bennet made her way from the middle to the outside of the row of the choir loft she was sitting in and slammed the door behind her. Mr. Bennet rose from his seat and chased after his wife. He looked back at Brother Bob and shrugged before escaping through the door leading to the back of the church.

The outburst shocked the congregation into silence. Brother Bob tried to use the last inch of dry fabric to blot the sweat on his red face. I wondered why he didn't just remove his jacket.

I snuck a look at Mrs. Jackson, and she sat like a statue, face forward, mouth still covered. I wondered if she could still breathe and envisioned her passing out and having to be revived. Church was never this exciting! Proof that God answered prayers.

"Let me continue. I planned for this passage and studied it long before yesterday's unfortunate letter. Afterward, the three of us at the preacher table reviewed our texts for today and noticed the Lord led all of us to this story. We took that as a direction from the Holy Spirit to preach it anyway."

Brother Bob seemed to grow in confidence as he searched the faces before him. "If you will, please turn to John 8. We'll be reading from verses 8-11."

Oh, good. A story. I scanned the story, reading along silently. There was a murmuring of amen when he finished, and I closed my Bible, settling in to hear how disobeying God leads us all straight to Hell.

"We are familiar with the commandment not to engage in adultery, and that adulterers will not inherit the Kingdom of God," Brother Bob explained.

We won't be seeing Mrs. Jackson in Heaven no matter how many Bible verses she knows. I smugly crossed my arms, remembering the times that she compared us unfavorably to *good* Christian children, like Bradley. A quick glance back to Derrick, who, I noticed, was chewing the nubs at the end of his fingers, completely uninterested in what Brother Bob said. Emily caught my eye and shrugged, pointing back at Derrick. He was missing all the good stuff.

Brother Bob stepped down from the pulpit to the floor. Standing between the two rows of pews, he let out a sad sigh, his tone soft and compassionate. "This is not a story about the consequences of adultery, alleged or otherwise. This story is a reminder that sometimes things are not as they seem. You've all said nothing exciting happens in Paradise Point, but that's not a good enough excuse to destroy the reputation of others for entertainment. How would you want to be treated? I feel confident there are some women in our community who have very strong opinions about what it's like to experience such a public humiliation, no matter how slight it seems. Let's not forget the humiliated woman came out on top in this story. It was the accusers who went away disappointed when Jesus revealed their sins. In writing, I might add."

I snuck a quick peek at Mrs. Jackson while I waited for the yelling about Hell to start. It didn't. Mrs. Jackson sat facing the front, and I saw a quick smile and "thank you" mouthed in Brother Bob's direction. I felt a little bad about what happened to her. But only a little.

After lunch, I spent the afternoon lying on the couch, reading in front of the box window fan. The hum made me sleepy. Mama had finished preparing for the week ahead and was in her chair reading when a thought popped into my head.

"Mama?"

"Um hmm?" she asked, not looking up from her book.

"Why didn't Brother Bob yell this morning the way he usually does?"

Mama put a bookmark in to hold her place and set the book in her lap. "Probably because it wasn't necessary. Sounds like you paid better attention without the yelling."

"But it seems like he really should have yelled at Mrs. Jackson. She thinks she's so perfect, and she should know better. I thought she knew all the verses in the Bible."

"Mrs. Jackson doesn't know all the verses in the Bible, just the ones she wants to use. Why are you interested in this, anyway?" Mama asked.

"You heard her at the Fine Christian Ladies Association meeting. She was so mean. I can't believe no one's done anything like this before. Why didn't you say anything?"

Mama sighed. "She is difficult, that's for sure. But like Brother Bob said, sometimes things aren't what they seem."

"Do you think she has a crush on Mr. Bennet? That's just gross." I wrinkled my nose.

"I think it's none of our business. That's for her and Mr. and Mrs. Bennet to sort out. I know this is entertaining for y'all, but be careful. You wouldn't want anyone to write anything about you in the newspaper, would you?"

"No, ma'am. I guess not. But I still think Mrs. Jackson deserved it," I said.

"Well, I suppose you're entitled to your opinion. But I expect you to keep that opinion to yourself. Understand?" she asked.

"Yes, ma'am."

Chapter 12

The town meeting was usually pretty full. This month it was unusually packed. When the good people of Paradise Point showed up at city hall, the sun hadn't yet set. The June heat made it almost unbearable. The windows and doors were open, and women were fanning themselves to ward off the heat and mosquitos.

Kids crowded the park, swarming and crawling all over the playground and beach area while they waited for their parents to attend the meeting. A few were playing some kind of game with a ball. It had complicated rules that changed depending on whoever was in charge. We didn't take part. Kids played basketball on the newly paved court. Others were taking turns alternating between the swings and merry-go-round, trying their hardest to fling each other off into the sand. Occasionally we'd hear the loud thunk of a kid thrown to the ground and shrieks of laughter from the ones lucky enough to hang on tight. Sweaty hands and slick metal bars were a terrible combination. It was a miracle none of us died during those long nights with no adult supervision.

A couple of kids sat at a picnic table, taking turns with a Rubik's Cube, arguing about the best way to get all sides single colors without pulling up the stickers and replacing them. There was always one kid with that suggestion in the group. We claimed our perch on the monkey bars so we could hear the grown-ups and get a better view of what was happening in the meeting.

"Jeez, it's so crowded people are standing in the doorway," Brian said.

"I know," Julie said. "My dad said this is going to be a good one. People are angry about the As Always letters and they want Mr. Johnson to do something about it."

"Yeah, but some people think it's great. My dad said it's the funniest thing that's ever happened here," Derrick said.

"I don't know what Mr. Johnson can do since he couldn't stop anyone from writing anything about his wife," Kevin said.

"But he didn't know about that letter before it was printed. Look." Charlie nodded toward the parking lot. "There's Miss Mary Lou."

Miss Mary Lou slammed the door to her ancient blue pickup and stomped her way toward the building.

"She looks like an angry bull ready to charge," Charlie said.

I giggled, imagining her pawing the ground with her hoof, head down, eyes red and angry, as she broke through the doors into the meeting.

"And Mrs. Johnson is sitting in the front with Mr. Johnson and Bradley," Julie said.

Bradley was the only kid in town to sit with their parents at the meetings.

"Do you think Mrs. Jackson will come?" Emily asked.

"Probably depends on if Mr. Bennet is here," Derrick answered.

We laughed, thinking it would be quite a show if all three of the ladies mentioned in the As Always letters were present at the same meeting. This night had a lot of entertainment potential, and we were here for it.

Mr. Johnson called the meeting to order and opened it with the recitation of the Pledge of Allegiance. The grown-ups stood and turned to face the yellowing, dusty flag standing in the room's corner and, with their hands over their hearts, said the words they had repeated countless times from memory. It was so ingrained in us, even as kids, that every one of us on the playground stopped what we were doing and put our hands on our hearts, doing the same.

When the grown-ups, who were lucky enough to have a seat, sat down, Mr. Johnson called Reverend Smith to the front to offer a quick prayer before the business officially began. He never asked Brother Bob to say the opening prayer. Everyone knew he prayed too long.

Reverend Smith stood and invited everyone to bow their heads, and they did. We didn't. Talking to God wasn't as automatic as pledging allegiance to the flag.

"God, thank you for the colorful people of Paradise Point and for allowing us to live in such a beautiful place. Thank you for friendships that have endured for generations. Guide our conversations as we discuss important matters. Help us compromise when necessary and think creatively as we solve problems, not create new ones."

We giggled.

"He's sneaky. Sounds like Mrs. Jackson's prayer," Emily said.

"We hope to leave here with friendships intact and a community that was better than before. Amen."

The grown-ups echoed his amen, and I caught that he used the phrase "better than before." It was like the "As Always, Here to Make You Better," at the end of the letters in the paper, but maybe not close enough to matter. *Would a preacher write the letters?* We had already decided it couldn't be Brother Bob. But who knew? It could be anyone.

The bars dug into our behinds, so we were swinging our weight from side to side. Sore butts were the price of not giving up our premium spot.

Mr. Johnson stood behind the podium again. Mrs. Johnson brought the community chest to the front of the room. She set it on a table next to the podium. Slips of paper stuffed into the chest so that the domed lid couldn't shut. A few brightly colored scraps fluttered to the ground when he opened the lid.

"Y'all might as well get comfortable," he joked. "Looks like we are going to be here awhile."

The town meeting rarely had a scheduled agenda. Paradise Point was small, and this system ensured everyone spoke their mind. Anyone in town could write an issue they wanted to discuss and put it into the chest anytime during the month. Then Mr. Johnson would draw the slips from the chest, and they gave every concern time for discussion until they settled it. This meant the meeting could last for hours. The citizens usually saved only the most important, or irritating, things to discuss at the meetings. No one wanted to be there all night. Tonight, of course, was the exception. Mr. Johnson wasn't exaggerating Saturday at the diner when he said there were a lot of concerns. People were on edge because of the letters. This meeting had the potential to be explosive.

Mr. Johnson reached for the slip on the floor. "I guess we'll start with this one." He unfolded the yellow scrap of paper. The creased paper made four small boxes.

From out of nowhere, a neon green and pink hacky sack hit Julie in the head.

"What the hell?" Julie rubbed her head.

"Shhh! Go over there," Emily said to the group, laughing as they resumed kicking the hacky sack. With each successful kick, there had been cheers and with each miss, trash talk. Their play was distracting our spying.

Some outsiders looked up from their journals at a picnic table and chuckled. One nodded at us and pointed to the hacky sack kickers who didn't want to tangle with Emily and had moved closer to the basketball court to play. He mentioned something to the woman sitting next to him and they laughed. I wondered if they were writers or artists. Why else would they have leatherbound journals and pens at the park?

Everywhere on Paradise Point, throughout the year, artists would sit in a spot for hours, sketching or painting. Mostly, they were invisible to us. We often had authors come and stay in cottages on the beach to write. Once, a man rented the apartment above the post office for six months. We rarely saw him, unless he walked the beach in the mornings while we rode our bikes to school. But you could hear him smacking keys on his typewriter through the open window for all hours of the day and night. I didn't hear it, but Miss Mary Lou and Miss Bessie said that he made all kinds of commotion in his room, moving furniture, singing, yelling at his characters, and acting crazy. Turns out, he was writing a horror film and went insane. At least that's what Miss Mary Lou told Miss Bessie.

Mayor Johnson's voice called my attention back to the meeting.

"There are no less than twenty-seven potholes that need filling on Pelican Drive. I have driven from end to end and am tired of having to run my Jeep into Ms. Richardson's yard every time I drive home from work."

The grown-ups sat still, waiting.

"Mrs. Evans, as you know, we will need to get bids and see if the budget will allow for it. All I can say for now is we'll see."

"That means no," Julie said, and we all nodded. There was a certain understanding that when a grown-up said, "We'll see," it always meant no.

"Well, you get some bids, or you'll see me send a bill to the city for new tires." Mrs. Evans nodded with arms crossed and a hearty humph.

Mr. Johnson pulled the next slip of paper. His eyes squinted, trying to make out the handwriting. He brought the paper closer to his face and then stretched his arm out again before reading.

"The 4th of July celebration committee has run amok. I've always had the fresh squeezed lemonade stand. And it's always in the spot right next to the beach seating for the fireworks. I understand this year that Ms. Richardson has allowed her cousin, that ne'er-do-well drunk, to have a lemonade stand right across from mine!"

Ms. Richardson jumped to her feet and yelled, "Who are you calling a 'ne'er-do-well drunk,' Annie? We know all about Jack and his recent trip to see about a business opportunity. Janie said she saw him picking up trash in a reflective vest on the lawn at Serenity Gardens, and he wasn't there for a job. At least not a paying one. Maybe worry about your own ne'er-do-well."

Mrs. Lambert stood, fists clenched, and faced Ms. Richardson. From across the room, she fired back, "Maybe Janie should mind her own damn business."

We stared wide-eyed at the spectacle unfolding as the two women moved toward each other. Ms. Richardson climbed over Miss Mary Lou's lap to get to the aisle and Mrs. Lambert tripped over Mrs. Johnson's purse on the floor, landing face-first in Brother Bob's lap. He jumped up, knocking her to the floor and, as quick as he could compose himself, reached down to help her to her feet. She smoothed her clothes and rushed toward Ms. Richardson in the aisle. Ms. Richardson picked up a folding chair propped up on the wall and held it in front of her as a shield. Mrs. Lambert swung, and her purse connected solidly with the metal chair.

"It's like the WWE," Brian shrieked with excitement.

"Too bad Hulk Hogan isn't here. Maybe you could get his autograph," Charlie joked.

The mood shifted, even on the playground. Everyone stopped playing. We focused on listening to the yelling and crashing sounds coming from the meeting as people tried to get out of the way. It was unsettling to see grown-ups behave this way.

A long, loud whistle broke through the melee and snapped everyone to attention. We watched as Miss Bessie stood on top of the table at the front of the room.

"Annie and Linda, what the hell are y'all doing? Get back in your seats. Annie, there will be two lemonade stands this year because you always run out. Deal with it. Linda, in the future, you can't decide that way. You are the president of the committee, not a dictator."

The mood settled a bit and the grown-ups returned to their seats, keeping some distance from both Ms. Richardson and Mrs. Lambert.

"If everyone has settled down, we can continue," Mr. Johnson said.

The next slip was some boring complaint about people leaving the public bathrooms at the park and marina a mess. There was a discussion about hiring someone to do routine checks and restocking.

After several other mundane requests and complaints that were solved easily, we were losing interest in the meeting. Our butts were hurting from the bars, and we were about to flip off and find something else to do when we heard Mr. Johnson laugh before reading the next slip.

"Wait to y'all hear this one," he said, catching his breath and wiping tears from his eyes.

"I am sick and tired of our police not assisting the citizens of Paradise Point. Three times I called to get help, and they refused me all three times. There is a roach, one of those flying ones, that has taken up residence in my house. Once, sitting right on my toilet seat when I lifted the lid. Imagine the horror! What if I had just sat down without checking? I'd have had a heart attack. Another time, it dive-bombed me when I was ironing my dress for church."

We shook with disgust at the thought of a crunchy roach landing in our hair. It was almost as bad as head lice.

"I called to have it removed and was told that is not a reason to call for a policeman and I needed to handle it myself. I ask why, since nothing ever happens in Paradise Point, do we need a policeman if they won't help me get rid of this roach? What are my taxes going for?" he read.

Mr. Johnson couldn't stop laughing, and it was infectious. People couldn't contain themselves at the absurdity of this request.

"Why doesn't she just kill the damn thing?" Charlie asked no one in particular.

"I know. Police are here to catch bad guys, not kill roaches," I said.

"To be fair, we don't have any bad guys in Paradise Point," Emily said.

And that was true, as far as we knew then.

Mr. Johnson set the slip on the pile of other resolved concerns. "Get some bug spray from Mr. Williams's grocery store. I'm sure he can help you find something suitable. Until then, get a broom and get rid of it yourself. And don't bother the police with such a ridiculous problem."

Mr. Johnson pulled another slip from the pile, unfolding it to reveal a half page. He smoothed it and, setting it on the podium, took a moment to read silently before clearing his throat.

"As everyone is aware, there is a poop problem in Paradise Point. Hopefully now Mayor Johnson will enact an ordinance that requires people to pick up after their dogs so they won't suffer public humiliation and the town won't smell like steaming dog shit on a hot day."

"That one's Mrs. Stewart's, I bet," I said.

"I second it," Miss Mary Lou shouted from her seat.

"Wait, that isn't how it works, Mary Lou," Mr. Johnson said.

"Yes, it is. Someone brought it up, and I second it. Now let's vote on it while everyone is here. We can finally get something done at one of these dreadful meetings," Miss Mary Lou said.

"She's right," Mrs. Stewart said, "and I'm sure there is plenty of support for the ordinance. Let's call for a vote."

Before Mr. Johnson could argue, she said, "All in favor of an ordinance, raise your hand."

She counted as nearly the entire room raised their hands.

"All those opposed." She waited and counted three hands. They were the same three who voted against any change in Paradise Point. Emily's mama was in that group.

"The preachers never vote, so it looks like the town has spoken and we need an ordinance." Miss Mary Lou smiled, obviously pleased with the outcome.

"All right. City Council will draft something for approval at the meeting next month. Mr. Carter, I assume you can have that ready?"

Mr. Carter nodded.

"And, Mr. Williams, will you consider building special boxes to hold dog poop bags near our public trash cans? Make a materials list with the projected cost and get it to the City Council as soon as possible."

"Sure, I can do that," Mr. Williams said.

"Speaking of the letters, I found this earlier in the week. I know it is out of the ordinary, but I think we should consider it."

Mr. Johnson pulled out a white envelope, the kind bills came to the house in through the mail. Mr. Johnson pulled out a piece of white paper and unfolded it, smoothing it on the top of the podium before clearing his throat and reading it out loud.

"Ms. Randall needs to be fired, and a suitable editor hired for the *Paradise Point Gazette*. She is inexperienced and allows anything in that paper to sell copies. There needs to be a full investigation into who is writing the As Always letters and why she has printed them. From the moment she arrived, she's messed everything up. I think we should boycott the paper as long as she prints such gossip about the people in our town."

"Finally, the good stuff," Derrick said.

Emily shushed the ball players next to us, and we shifted to get some relief from our aching behinds.

A loud murmur rose from the group as they discussed this letter with the people in their vicinity. Each conversation was indiscernible to us, but we could tell from the body language that some people were all for it.

I scanned the room, looking for Miss Mary Lou, Mrs. Johnson, and Mrs. Jackson's reaction. All three of them sat with their arms crossed, watching the crowd, kind of like we were.

"Do you think they wrote that suggestion?" Julie asked, moving from side to side.

"Maybe." I lifted one thigh at a time to relieve some of the pressure of the bars.

"That makes sense," Charlie said. "Since all the letters were about them. They'd all be mad at Ms. Randall for printing them. She had to have read them first."

"And she could have at least warned them," Brian said. "Isn't she friends with Miss Mary Lou?"

I thought back to my haircut. It seemed like they were friends. Brian had a point.

"Quiet down," Mr. Johnson called out over all the conversation. "We'll open the floor for discussion."

"I can see where you'd like Ms. Randall fired, especially since she embarrassed Julia," someone called out.

"Before we talk about firing Ms. Randall, we should give her the opportunity to speak for herself." Mr. Johnson nodded toward Ms. Randall. She had been taking notes during the meeting for the paper.

"I have nothing to add. Anyone can write anything they want in the Letter to the Editor page," Ms. Randall said.

"Makes sense," Kevin said. "How is she supposed to know how everyone will react?"

Ms. Randall continued, "If you don't like it, maybe you should move. It sounds like most of you don't like your neighbors, anyway."

The room erupted.

"Us move? Why don't you move? Coming in here and stirring up trouble like that," Miss Mary Lou yelled. "I nearly lost my business because of you."

"And poor Mrs. Jackson's reputation was near about ruined," Mrs. Johnson said rising from her seat and moving toward where Ms. Randall sat.

"And Mrs. Bennet can't leave the house, and there wasn't even a letter written about her," Mrs. Jackson said.

It was the first time we had heard Mrs. Jackson speak since the letter.

"I understand you ladies are mad. Maybe I would be, too. But that's not my fault. I only printed the letters that were sent in. If you notice, I printed others last week. At least some of your friends and neighbors appreciate the letters," Ms. Randall said.

"You think there will be another fight?" Brian asked.

"I don't know," I said.

"I hope so. Nothing exciting ever happens in Paradise Point. Two fights in one night would be awesome," Brian said.

"I hope they don't," Julie said. "They're all acting crazy."

We watched as Mr. Johnson tried to regain control of the meeting.

Brother Bob stood and made his way to the podium. Mr. Johnson stepped back, giving him the floor.

"Here he goes. He's gonna tell them they're goin' straight to Hell if they don't stop," Derrick said.

Another loud whistle from Miss Bessie brought the crowd under control and silence settled over the room.

"Proverbs 26:20-21 reminds us that 'Without wood, a fire goes out; without a gossip, a quarrel goes down. As charcoal to embers and as wood to fire, so is a quarrelsome person for kindling strife.'"

Brother Bob paused, and the grown-ups got quiet.

"Reverend Smith prayed earlier for unity and enduring friendships. There is a strong history among many of you. These letters have brought unresolved hurts and betrayals from the past to light. Ms. Randall is right. She isn't responsible for what someone else writes. Your quarrel shouldn't be with her. It should be with each other for the way you continue to gossip throughout the week about each letter."

The tension eased as the grown-ups relaxed into their seats. It surprised me there was no mention of Hell in his mini sermon.

"This is a caring community, and I know you have it within you to let these letters run their course. You'll see. Soon the town will be back to normal. Firing Ms. Randall will solve nothing. Besides, that would be the Becketts' decision, anyway."

He turned to Ms. Randall. "Is there anything you'd like to say?"

"Y'all won't believe the next letter!"

Chapter 13

Dropping such a bomb threw the grown-ups into a tizzy. Arguments popped off like the Fourth of July fireworks we watched every year from the beach.

"Look." Emily pointed to the side door. "Ms. Randall's sneaking out!"

We stretched and strained our necks to see around the corner of the building, and sure enough, Ms. Randall had slipped away unnoticed during the melee. She turned nervously, looking right at us, and put her fingers to her lips as she disappeared behind the building.

Miss Mary Lou wasn't far behind and stopped the hacky sack kids to see if they had seen Ms. Randall. No one ratted her out, and Miss Mary Lou roared out of the parking lot in her old blue pickup. Mr. Williams came running out of the meeting just as the dust settled behind her.

Over the arguing and speculation, we heard Mr. Lewis and Mr. Carter laughing at the spectacle.

"Look at them. Laughing their damn heads off," Kevin said.

By now, the shock had worn off, and we were laughing too. Every grown-up in town had fussed at us for misbehaving in public, and tonight they were the ones yelling, lying, gossiping, and fighting!

Julie's parents came first and called her off the monkey bars.

"Gotta go." She flipped off, landing on her feet. "Let me know what happens," she called out and ran across the park to her parents.

One by one, we were called by our parents to go home. It was late, but as we got into our car, I noticed that the couple at the picnic table were still there, chuckling and writing furiously in their notebooks.

For the rest of the week, all anyone talked about was the next letter. In Mr. Williams's store, I overheard two ladies discussing the possibility it could be about Ms. Randall. They wondered if she was in some kind of trouble.

Julie said every customer in her dad's restaurant had a different idea. Maybe someone in the bank was stealing money. There was a new teller who just moved into town. The one who let a little too much of her cleavage show as she helped customers. Maybe it was to distract them so they wouldn't notice their deposits and withdrawals were short?

Or maybe it was Dr. Sheridan's wife. She'd been acting strange ever since her surgery. And she had access to his locked medicine cabinet. Perhaps she was helping herself to more than just her prescription?

The theories were getting wilder by the minute. But we wouldn't have to wait much longer.

I ran into Miss Bessie at the Jiffy store. Mama gave me an extra dollar to clean the house. I couldn't wait to spend it on *Pac-Man*. I had enough quarters to play for an hour as long as no one else wanted to play. If they did, then Ms. Richardson would make me share.

"You all right?" Miss Bessie held the door for me.

"Yes, ma'am."

"Why are you rubbing your shoulder?"

"Oh, *Pac-Man*. I guess I just got a little too into it," I explained.

"I see. Well, tell your mama I said hi. And, if you're coming to the diner on Saturday, y'all better get there early. I imagine it's going to be packed. It seems like Ms. Randall will do anything to sell a paper."

"Yes, ma'am," I said. "Wait, Miss Bessie?"

"What?"

"Everyone seems to think they know who's writing the letters. Who do you think it is?"

Miss Bessie smiled, a twinkle in her eye. "I imagine it's someone who likes things to be done in a particular and proper way. See you Saturday."

I rolled her words over and over in my mind. *Where had I heard that before? Miss Mary Lou!* She said that Miss Bessie was very particular. She wanted things done in a certain way. Like making us put our bikes in the bike rack. And Miss Bessie knew everything about everyone because she was always at the diner and everyone else was always hanging around the diner. Julie said all the customers in her dad's restaurant gossiped while they ate. We'd heard plenty of gossip at the diner, too. I had to take this to the group.

Friday afternoon, we convened at the community pool. We relented and let a few mamas slather us in sunscreen. Evidently, our mamas found out we had never opened the sunscreen they put in our bags the entire summer. We were sure the other mamas told on us.

"Hold still. I won't get it in your eyes," Mrs. Rodgers said to Charlie as he tried to wiggle away.

"It stings," he whined.

"Carrie, you're next." Mrs. Rodgers motioned me over as Charlie broke away and jumped into the deep end, far out of her reach.

Reluctantly, I handed her the sunscreen Mama threw into my bag. I couldn't stand sunscreen. Still can't.

"Carrie, turn around," she said.

I turned obediently, so she could slather sunscreen on my shoulders and back, and willed her to hurry. I needed to join the others in the deep end to tell them who I thought wrote the letters.

"It stinks." I wrinkled my nose.

"It does not," Mrs. Rodgers said. "That's it. Now go on," she added, snapping the lid closed. "Which is your bag?"

"The purple one," I yelled just before launching myself headfirst into the pool.

We gathered in the corner of the deep end near the ladder. The pool was quiet. Families with little kids had left already. They still had nap times. At twelve, no one made us take naps. It would be several years before we realized the value of a nap.

"Okay," I heard Brian say. "My dad said he is sure it's Miss Bessie."

I was stunned. *Brian stole my thunder!* I wanted to tell them my theory first.

"Why does he think it's Miss Bessie?" I asked.

"Keep your voice down." Emily looked around to see if any of the mamas were listening to us gossip. We'd be in trouble for sure if we got caught gossiping like the grown-ups.

"Because it's bringing people into the diner," Brian explained. "Think about all the money she's making since the letters."

It was true. Anytime we rode our bikes past the diner, it was full. No matter the time of day. Before, it had a strong morning crowd and a few regulars at lunch. But now, she was full all the time and even stayed open later to accommodate the lingering crowds.

"My dad ran into her at Mr. Williams's grocery store. She said her supplier couldn't keep up with the demand and since she only gets a shipment once a week, she had to supplement with local groceries. It was expensive, but she was making a fortune lately," Brian explained.

I wanted to add to the conversation, but this was the missing piece. It wasn't enough that she was particular about things, but this financial windfall was confirmation that I was on to the right person.

"My dad says the restaurant business is tough. Maybe she needed to make more money," Julie said.

"Maybe, but what is she going to do, write letters about everyone in town? Then what?" I asked.

We quietly treaded water, considering what this could mean.

"Do you think she'll write a letter about us?" Kevin asked.

"She's always fussin' at us about leaving our bikes on the ground by the front door," I said.

"And leaving the table a mess," Julie said.

"And eating the same 'unhealthy' breakfast every Saturday," Derrick added.

"What if the next letter is about us?" Brian asked. "Will we get in trouble?"

"Don't be ridiculous." Emily splashed him in the face. "None of the letters so far have been about kids. There are kids way worse than us. For instance, that obnoxious Bradley. Or Whitney. She wrecked her mom's car. Or Todd. He pulled the Coke machine in front of the gas station over, trying to shake one out. Don't worry, no one is going to write a letter about us."

But I wasn't too sure. I bet none of the people who had been in the letters thought they were so closely observed and judged, either.

Chapter 14

There was a flaw in our theory. I couldn't believe we didn't think about it before.

I was on the porch swing, working my way through the latest summer reading selection. I'd already read more than half the list. *Harriet the Spy* was the twelfth book I'd read that summer. It was a shame they only suggested twenty books. Every year, my teachers reminded me these were suggestions, but a list was a list. A list of books was the best list of all.

The idea struck when I was deep into my reading session and interrupted the story.

How would Miss Bessie know the letters would bring in more business? That wasn't a guarantee.

I set my book down on my chest. That meant she didn't write the first letter. But she could have seen how it directed business to her and written the other letters.

I dangled my left leg over the side of the porch swing. The toe of my well-worn sneaker just barely gripped the gray-painted porch boards. I pushed off and felt the swing move gently back and forth. Careful not to roll off, I reflected on the last few weeks.

Miss Bessie had connections with Mrs. Johnson, Miss Mary Lou, and Mrs. Jackson. And she laughed the loudest at the letters. There was no love lost between her and Mrs. Johnson or Mrs. Jackson, but she and Miss Mary Lou were friends.

The heat of the lazy summer afternoon made it increasingly hard to concentrate, and the gentle swaying of the swing rocked me to sleep.

"Got her," Derrick yelled as I awoke abruptly, flailing my arms and trying to stop the flow of water into my face.

"What the hell, Derrick," I sputtered, reaching out in front of me and rolling right off the comfy swing. I landed on my hands and knees with a thud into a slippery puddle.

Charlie, Derrick, Kevin, and Brian responded with peals of laughter, loud enough to wake the dead.

"I told you a squirt gun wouldn't wake her up," Derrick said.

I wiped the water from my eyes and opened them to see Kevin, Brian, and Charlie had squirt guns, but what had done the damage was Derrick and the hose!

"Stop it, you idiots!" I yelled as I tried to get behind a chair, using it as a shield. That's when I saw my soggy copy of *Harriet the Spy* on the porch under the swing.

"Dammit! Look what y'all did," I yelled, picking up my book and assessing the damage. "Mrs. Wilson's gonna kill me! I'm telling her y'all did this." I shook the book, trying to get as much water off as I could. Mama would kill me, too. I was supposed to be careful with books.

"She won't kill you," Kevin said. "She just won't let you check out books for a while."

"Same thing to Carrie," Charlie said.

"Well, the damage is done anyway." Derrick started toward the porch with the hose.

I heard the spray start from the hose before Emily rode up, hollering something as she dropped her bike in my front yard.

Derrick turned, hose still spraying, and soaked her to the bone.

Now it was on!

The boys laughed as they moved across the grass toward their next target. Emily wasn't having any of it and charged at them. I looked around and put the book in the only dry place I could find: the steps leading into the house. Head down, Emily was running right for the boys with her arm outstretched, trying to shield the water from her face.

Thinking quickly, I jumped off the porch and ran to the spigot on the side of the house, giving it a quick turn, ending the deluge pointed in Emily's direction.

"Hey!" Derrick yelled, looking down at the trickle at the end of the hose, just as Emily pushed him to the ground.

"Whoa! That's enough!" Reverend Smith hollered from the yard next door.

The argument ceased suddenly. We'd never heard Reverend Smith raise his voice.

"What's going on?" he demanded, walking the short distance in record time. He reached over and helped Emily and Derrick to their feet, careful not to get himself wet. He collected the squirt guns from the other boys before turning to me.

"Carrie, come and wind this hose back up. And go get some towels. Y'all need to clean up the porch before your parents get home."

"Yes, sir," I said, and did as I was told.

I came outside with an armful of colorful beach towels as Reverend Smith directed the others to the steps.

"I don't know what's going on here. I assume a bit of fun got out of hand, but fighting is unacceptable. Boys, you know better than to fight with girls, although Emily looked like she could hold her own. You're lucky neither one of you got hurt. Now, let's get up there and clean up this mess before all of y'all get in trouble."

We stood there like idiots while Reverend Smith walked toward my front porch, still amazed that he had inserted himself into the situation.

"Well, don't just stand there. Let's go." He motioned we should follow him.

Derrick and Emily brushed off the dirt and grass as best they could and followed the group toward the porch.

Reverend Smith handed out the towels and took the last one for himself.

I looked at him curiously. "Umm. Don't worry about it. We can clean it up."

"I know you can," he said.

"Usually, when we make a mess, our parents make us clean," I explained. Reverend Smith wasn't married and didn't have any kids, so maybe he didn't know the rules about parents making their kids clean as punishment.

"I'm sure they do. But I am not your parents," he said.

Reverend Smith smiled and gave directions, giving each of us a task and an area to clean. He wiped down the swing and wrung out the cushions before flopping them over the railing to dry.

We sloshed our wet towels around, eyeing him suspiciously.

"So, would anyone like to tell me what this was all about?" he asked.

We were quiet.

"Come on," he coaxed. "When I went inside next door, Carrie was napping peacefully on the swing. Then I come out to a fight in the yard. And I'm pretty sure I heard cussing."

Our eyes widened as we glanced at one another.

"Are you going to tell on us?" Emily asked.

"No, I don't think that's necessary." Reverend Smith chuckled.

The story tumbled out. I was sleeping, and they sprayed me with water, making me fall out of the swing and ruin my library book. The boys tried to defend themselves, saying they were bored and thought it was a funny prank.

"Emily, that leaves you. How do you fit into all of this?" he asked.

"I was coming over to tell Carrie something," she said nervously.

"And what was that?" Reverend Smith asked, righting an upturned flowerpot and putting the soil that was dumped out back in.

"Um, well..." Emily hesitated, giving the rest of us a worried look.

"Well, what?" Reverend Smith asked, moving to the next pot that took a tumble.

Emily took a deep breath. "Well, someone covered the newspaper office in fish guts."

"What?" Reverend Smith turned quickly, knocking the pot back on its side.

"Yeah, I was on my way to play *Pac-Man*. I found some quarters under the sofa when I vacuumed, and I thought since it's hot and everyone else was busy, I'd have the game to myself."

"What about the fish guts?" Reverend Smith asked.

"Oh, yeah, anyway, I turned onto Main Street and there was a crowd of people there and oh my God, the smell," she said. "Oh, sorry, I shouldn't say 'oh my God' in front of you." Her face flushed.

"You shouldn't say it at all, but go on," Reverend Smith said.

"I pulled up on my bike and heard Miss Mary Lou say, 'Serves that heifer right,' and some other people agreed," Emily said, her voice strong and quick with the delight of new gossip.

Then just as quickly, she dropped her gaze. "Oops, um. Sorry. I'm not supposed to gossip in front of you either."

Rolling his eyes, Reverend Smith said, "You aren't supposed to gossip at all."

"Well, anyway, I was coming to tell Carrie and then the boys were here, and I guess you know the rest."

"I'm just curious. Why were you coming to tell Carrie?" he asked.

"Because I wondered if that will be in the next letter. Maybe it—"

We interrupted her with a loud "SHHH!" We didn't want Reverend Smith to know we'd *all* been gossiping. There was nothing we could do for Emily, but we had the good sense to know we needed to stay in the preacher's good graces to get into Heaven.

She stopped and Reverend Smith sat on the steps, motioning for us to sit down as well. The porch was pretty well dried, and we were wet anyway, so we obeyed, readying ourselves for a lecture about gossiping and Hell and all the rest of it.

"Let's talk about the letters. Y'all have been in the diner every Saturday, and I'm sure it's entertaining. Maybe even a little unsettling to know that someone is watching and judging, and then writing about what they see. It's tempting, even for me, to talk about it during the week." Reverend Smith took a breath and looked each of us directly in the eye.

"But it wouldn't be right." Then, with a distinct twinkle in his eye, he added, "Even though it's fun."

The group let out a collective exhale. After all, weren't going to Hell. Reverend Smith was an ally. He thought gossip was fun!

"Now, go get dried off, and don't track all that in your houses or your mamas will have your behinds. Kevin, I'll see you in church on Sunday."

And that's how Reverend Smith became our favorite grown-up in town.

Chapter 15

News of the fish guts spread through Paradise Point like wildfire. And, like they had all summer, everyone had a theory.

The next day, we sorted out clues on top of the monkey bars.

"Maybe it was Miss Mary Lou. She was there and had called Ms. Randall a heifer," Emily said.

"Or, could be Mrs. Johnson or Mrs. Jackson," I said. "Any one of them could still be furious with her. She did print the letters." Although we thought it was unlikely that either of them would touch fish guts. They were too prissy.

"My mama said she thought it was Joe Miller's wife. Finally caught on about everything," Kevin said. "And she has access to all the fish guts she wants, and she isn't afraid to touch them."

Joe Miller was a fishing guide and people around town had long suspected he and Ms. Randall were more than just friends.

"No way. No lady is going to put fish guts on the newspaper steps. Too gross for them," Derrick offered.

Julie, Emily, and I agreed. This time, the boys were right. We might go along with all kinds of things to prove ourselves, but we'd draw the line at handling fish guts.

"I bet someone knows who did it, and we'll read about it tomorrow," Brian said.

"No, you idiot! The paper is more than likely ready to be delivered. It will be at least a week before we find out who did it," Emily said.

"Oh yeah, I guess you're right," Brian said. "But maybe tomorrow someone in the diner will know something. People will still talk about it."

"Maybe," Julie said as her watch alarm beeped. "Shoot! I've gotta go. I'm supposed to be at the restaurant in a few minutes." She flipped off the bars and ran to her bike. "I'll meet you in the morning and let you know if I overhear anything," she yelled back before taking off.

The rest of the afternoon was a blur of *Pac-Man* and Coke Icee. Today there was an unexpected upset, and Emily's initials were at the top of the high score screen beating both Julie and Derrick's previous scores.

"That's only because you played all day yesterday." Derrick sulked.

"Quit your whining. You're still in second place," Brian said.

"I'd be higher if Ms. Richardson hadn't kicked us out for being loud," Derrick said. "I just needed one more turn!"

"It's just as well. I'm out of quarters," Charlie said. "I gotta get home, anyway."

Our bikes were in a tangle next to the ice machine where we'd dropped them earlier. My yellow bike was on the bottom, and I complained about everyone being careful not to scratch it, when I noticed something, or someone, on the porch of the newspaper office. As the others argued about *Pac-Man* and sorting out the bikes, I focused my gaze on the building down the street. I left the others to sort out the bike situation, and using the ice machine as cover, peeked around, trying to get a closer look. Someone was acting suspiciously at the steps. I ducked out of sight as the person turned and looked in our direction. Thinking the coast was clear, I peeked around the corner again and saw Bradley messing with the bottom of the door.

He stood up and turned to look around before calmly walking away.

"Carrie, are you gonna pick up your bike or what?" Charlie asked.

"Y'all will not believe this! I just saw Bradley leave something for Ms. Randall!" I was giddy with new gossip.

"What are you talking about?" Emily demanded, walking to where I stood and looking in the newspaper's direction. "There isn't anyone there."

"Not now, but while y'all were trash-talkin' about *Pac-Man* and arguing over the bikes, I saw Bradley kneel and mess around with something by the bottom of the door."

By now, all six of us were looking intently in that direction, as if willing Bradley to appear again.

"What are we standing around here for? Let's go see what he left," Derrick said, already on his bike.

We followed Derrick and were disappointed when we arrived. The fish guts were gone, but the smell wasn't.

"Yuck, that stinks." Emily wrinkled her nose.

"Maybe he was trying to clean it up?" Kevin said.

"Nope, it's a fresh empty bag." Derrick put the lid back on the trash can by the sidewalk.

"Then what was he doing here?" Charlie asked.

"Y'all, look here," I said, my nose up against the glass.

They crowded around me, and now there were six noses pushed up against the cool glass. There, on the floor, was a white envelope addressed in Bradley's perfect handwriting to Ms. Randall, editor of the *Paradise Point Gazette*.

Chapter 16

We packed into the diner the next morning. People stood outside, waiting to get in. Longtime residents and outsiders alike, everyone was trying to get in to hear if there was a new letter. I guess it never occurred to anyone in Paradise Point to buy their own paper. Or maybe it's just that there wasn't anything else to do most of the time. We were as excited as if it were Christmas morning. The whole of Paradise Point was buzzing with anticipation and gossip. Not only was there talk about the fish guts in front of the newspaper office, but we were all hopeful there would be a new letter.

Our bikes carefully stowed in the rack, we scurried into the diner and looked around. There wasn't a table available in the place. Miss Bessie waved us over to the counter and offered the floor in front of the dessert display case. It would be inconvenient, but beggars couldn't be choosers and we wanted to be there.

"Careful where you sit, kids," Miss Bessie said, as she passed by with a tray full of coffee and her famous cinnamon rolls. "I haven't mopped."

"It's all right," I said, and settled in the corner between Charlie and Emily.

"I'll be by shortly with your chocolate milk and cinnamon rolls. You'll have to be patient. It's busier than usual. I might have to expand and put tables out on the sidewalk," she said with a smile. Yes, business was booming.

"Yes, ma'am," we said, unsure she heard us over the conversations in the diner. Hopefully, she didn't tell our mamas we hadn't said "Yes, ma'am." One of the worst things a kid could do in Paradise Point was forget to say "Yes, ma'am" or "No, ma'am."

Julie looked around and leaned into the group. "Okay. It has to be Miss Bessie. It was never this busy before the letters."

"Oww! Watch it." Derrick shook his hand and blew on his fingers.

"Oops, sorry. I didn't see you," Jeremy said. He worked for Miss Bessie on the weekends and in the afternoons. "You shouldn't be sitting there, anyway."

"Miss Bessie told us to sit here, and you should mind your own business and do your job, not stepping on our fingers." Emily reached out to examine Derrick's hand.

Jeremy ignored us and delivered the tray of coffee and assorted breakfast orders to diners sitting in chairs at tables.

"Looks fine." Emily dropped Derrick's hand.

"How would you know?" Derrick asked, still shaking his hand a bit.

"Her grandpa's a vet. She knows stuff," Brian said.

"Her grandpa knows things about dogs and cats," Derrick whined.

"Quit whining, you're fine," Julie interrupted.

Our chocolate milk and cinnamon rolls arrived. Jeremy followed Miss Bessie with a red plastic milk crate and set it upside down in the middle of our group.

"Kids, I'm gonna leave this tray with you. It'll be like a little table. Try not to make a mess. Set it on the counter when you finish eating. Jeremy," she turned to look behind her, "steer clear of them when you come around that corner. I don't need any broken fingers."

"Now you tell him." Derrick winced, and Jeremy shot him an apologetic look.

"I said I was sorry," Jeremy said under his breath as he grabbed the next order to deliver.

"So, we're all convinced it's Miss Bessie?" I asked between mouthfuls.

Everyone nodded, and we downed the chocolate milk and cinnamon rolls in record time. No one dared spill a drop, lest Miss Bessie decide to write a letter about us, too.

The bells over the door chimed and in walked Bradley with a stack of the *Paradise Point Gazette* tucked under his arm.

"Look at him grinning like an idiot. What do you think he wrote in the letter to Ms. Randall?" Emily asked.

"It's probably about you." Julie licked the sticky cinnamon roll glaze from her fingers. "You should've been nicer to him."

I wondered if soon we'd read a letter about Julie that Emily wrote.

Kevin had just leaned in between the girls to add his two cents when Mr. Lewis stood to read.

"Ahem." He cleared his throat loudly and repeated himself three times, each one louder than before, until the crowd settled.

"Bradley, hand one of those papers to me. No need to put them all in the bin. I'll put the money in later," Mr. Lewis said.

"Everyone heard that, right?" Mr. Carter joked. "Don't worry, Bradley, I'll make sure he pays for it."

Bradley handed Mr. Lewis the paper on the top of the stack and sent a look our way. I couldn't read his face. Was he mad, happy, maybe conspiring about something? I smiled back, afraid to bring a letter on about myself, and he looked a little confused. He gave a quick wave and rushed out the door to finish his deliveries.

"What was that?" Emily hissed across our circle.

"Nothing," I answered, worried Emily might write a letter about me.

"Well, don't forget your little crush already delivered a letter. A smile and wave won't stop whatever he wrote," Emily said.

"Ew! Shut up, Emily! I don't have a crush on Bradley." I raised my voice to the loudest whisper I could muster. I didn't want the whole diner to start a rumor that I had a crush on Bradley Johnson. There was no telling what could end up in the *Paradise Point Gazette*, and Ms. Randall didn't seem above publishing dumb letters about crushes.

"Both of y'all shut up," Charlie said. "Mr. Lewis is fixin' to read."

Thankful for the reprieve, I settled against the wall holding up the counter. My heart pounded with anticipation and too much sugar.

"Well, this week's edition is even thicker than last week." Mr. Lewis held it out in front of him as if to weigh it.

"Get on with it," Ms. Richardson said.

Mr. Lewis made a terrific show of opening the pages and setting aside the sections that were of no interest.

"Lots of real estate listings. Anyone need a house?" he asked with a twinkle in his eye before setting it down on the table.

"Oh, what is this? The county is improving the highway fifteen miles from here. Anyone want to know about that?"

He set the county section on top of the real estate section.

"Looks like there is an entire section devoted to the 4th of July celebration. Seems to be all-hands-on-deck for this. Expecting an enormous crowd. If you aren't sure what you signed up for, I can pass this around so you can check." Mr. Lewis passed the section to the preacher table.

Brother Bob opened it, and nodding, passed it to Reverend Smith.

"Anyone need a kitten? Mrs. Anderson is looking for suitable homes for six—wow, that's a lot of kittens—in the want ads. Anyone?" He turned from side to side, making eye contact with other diners. "No homes for the poor little kittens?"

"Come on, give the people what they want," Mr. Carter said.

"Okay, here we are. Wow, someone in this room is going to be even more upset than Bill was a few weeks ago."

Mr. Lewis snapped the pages open and looked over the top of the newspaper in our direction, and I swear he winked at us.

Oh no, I thought. *Here it comes. We are gonna be in so much trouble about whatever they wrote.*

I looked nervously at my friends and could tell they were thinking the same thing. We were bracing ourselves for whatever Miss Bessie wrote.

"To Whom it May Concern," Mr. Lewis began. "There is a favorite dining establishment in this town that boasts an award-winning, and top-secret recipe for its cinnamon rolls. I have it on good authority that those award-winning rolls Miss Bessie likes to brag about are none other than store-bought cinnamon rolls from a can. That's why she can't share the recipe. She doesn't know what it is."

A collective gasp sucked the air out of the room as all heads turned toward Miss Bessie. Miss Bessie's face turned beet red. I'm pretty sure smoke was coming out of her ears like in cartoons.

"I knew it!" Mrs. Johnson yelled from a booth in the back. "All those years you made me buy those rolls at six dollars a dozen for the Fine Christian Ladies Association meeting because you wouldn't share the recipe. Said it was Grandma's recipe. Grandma's recipe, my ass!"

We watched, horrified, as Miss Bessie rushed out from behind the counter and headed in Mr. Lewis's direction.

"Oww!" Derrick yelled and shook his hand again. In her haste, Miss Bessie stepped on his fingers and didn't even stop to check on him.

"What the hell, Derrick?" Kevin said. "Even Brian isn't stupid enough to get his hand stepped on twice!"

I looked at Emily, her eyes huge at what we were seeing, as Julie said, "It wasn't about us!"

Mrs. Johnson got to Mr. Lewis first and yanked the paper from his hands, tearing off part of the page.

"Give me that!" Miss Bessie insisted and reached for the paper. Unfortunately, Mrs. Johnson stepped to the side quickly and turned her back just as Miss Bessie reached for the paper and, in the process, hit Mr. Lewis square in the face.

The air was still for a split second before the diner erupted in shouting and laughter. Mr. Lewis, shocked at what had just occurred, took a moment to check his face before standing and tipping his chair into the table, knocking off the tray Jeremy had precariously set down as he went to help Miss Bessie. The clatter of silverware and glass hitting the tile floor shocked the room into silence.

"I said, give me that paper," Miss Bessie hissed at Mrs. Johnson.

"I will." Mrs. Johnson moved to hand the paper to Miss Bessie, before jerking it back and saying, "After we read the rest of the letter."

Mrs. Johnson moved around the room, weaving in and out of tables, as Miss Bessie chased her.

She continued reading. "You've been overpaying by three or four times what you could have purchased for yourselves at Mr. Williams's grocery store. There is no shame in store-bought cinnamon rolls, as long as they taste good. As far as I know, the people at the bakery don't know they are sitting on an award-winning recipe. If they did, maybe they'd charge as much as Miss Bessie. As Always, Here to Make You Better."

"Get out now!" Miss Bessie bellowed over the laughter coming from the crowd, finally reaching Mrs. Johnson, who dropped the paper on her way out the front door.

The bells were jingling constantly with the flood of people trying to get away from Miss Bessie as fast as possible.

"I always thought there was something off about those rolls," Mrs. Anderson said.

"Every year. Every year, she enters them in the bake-off and no one noticed? We need new judges," Mrs. Rodgers said as she squeezed through the door.

"All of y'all get out! And don't let the door hit your ass on your way!" Miss Bessie called after the last of the crowd made their way to the door.

In her rush to get to the kitchen, she hadn't seen us still sitting on the floor in the corner. We were stunned at the spectacle, unsure if we should move.

"It can't be true," Charlie whispered. "The canned ones my mama makes don't taste like Miss Bessie's."

"That's because your mama gets the off brand," Emily said.

"Don't Miss Bessie and Mrs. Johnson have the same grandma?" Kevin asked.

"No. Their grandmas were sisters," I said. "But that explains why Mrs. Johnson was pissed about not getting the recipe."

"Yeah," Emily said. "I thought she was just cheap and didn't want to pay so much to pass off homemade cinnamon rolls as her own. She never brings them to the Fine Christian Ladies Association meetings in a box from the diner."

"But no one's fooled. Mama says every month she brings them, and they let her think they don't notice," Emily said.

"Shh," Charlie said, motioning behind the counter.

The noise from the pots and pans being slammed around had stopped, and we heard a weird muffled noise from the back. Derrick leaned against the wall and peeked around the counter to look back into the kitchen before returning to our little huddle and whispering, "I think Miss Bessie's crying."

Chapter 17

"It's not Miss Bessie," Julie whispered.

"Nope, not with that reaction," Emily said.

"Where's Jeremy?" I asked.

"He got the hell out of here with everyone else," Derrick said. "Amazingly, without stepping on my fingers."

We ignored Derrick's last comment. If you're gonna be dumb, you gotta be tough. How many times did one person need to have their fingers stepped on before they moved their hand?

The muffled noises from the kitchen were getting louder.

"She's coming. What should we do?" Charlie asked.

"Shh." Emily put her finger to her lips.

We scooted as tight as we could into the corner, pushing our backs flat against the wall. Miss Bessie hesitated at the counter above our heads, releasing a jagged sigh before the tears started again. We held our breath, unsure what she'd do if she caught us. Miss Bessie wasn't our favorite person, but sometimes she did nice things. She put the bike rack up for us. Every Saturday, she had our cinnamon rolls and chocolate milk ready. And she usually let us have the big booth so we could all fit.

But she was also a pain and bossy. She'd tell our mamas if we did anything, and I mean anything, wrong.

Miss Bessie walked from behind the counter and made her way to the front door. She turned the lock and flipped the Open, Come on In sign to Closed, Come Again Soon. There was nowhere for us to hide when she turned around to put the diner back in order.

"What are y'all still doing here? I told everyone to leave."

"Miss Bessie, we're sorry. We couldn't get up and out when all the, well, commotion happened with the letter," Emily said.

We scrambled to our feet, and Brian accidentally knocked over the tray we were using as a table. Glasses and sticky plates tumbled to the floor.

"Damn it, Brian," Julie said, and then, realizing what she'd said, looked over at Miss Bessie. "I mean, dang it, Brian, quit making a mess."

Miss Bessie laughed. "You know, I always say that sometimes there is no substitute for a well-placed cuss word."

"You won't tell Mama?" Julie asked suspiciously. This was a new side to Miss Bessie. We were used to Miss Mary Lou keeping our secrets, not Miss Bessie.

"No, I won't tell your mama."

"Miss Bessie, I don't care what anyone says. Your canned cinnamon rolls taste way better than the ones Mama gets at Mr. Williams's grocery store," Charlie said.

"Shut up, Charlie." I gave him a strong nudge in the ribs.

"Oww," he yelped, rubbing his side.

Miss Bessie ignored Charlie's comment and moved chairs away from the table nearest the door. "Carrie, grab that tub and rag behind the counter and bring it to me, please. This place is a disaster."

I jumped into action, thankful for something to do and hoping that Miss Bessie would elaborate.

Without being asked, the others followed my lead and started moving the chairs away from all the tables. Miss Bessie took the rag and tub and started to clean the first table.

We all worked in silence for a few minutes before Miss Bessie said, "Don't y'all have something more fun to do than clean up the diner? I can get all this put away."

"No, ma'am. We can help you." Brian brought an empty bin for the next table and took the full one from Miss Bessie to put on the counter.

"Well, make sure your helping doesn't cause a bigger mess." Miss Bessie winked at Brian, who returned a smile. This was the Miss Bessie we were used to.

"Carrie, get the broom and Charlie, follow her with the dustpan. Emily, you and Derrick take the dirty dishes and soak them in hot, soapy water in the kitchen. Kevin and Brian, you can get a bucket of hot and soapy water to help me wipe down the tables. Julie and I need you to mop and put the chairs back under the tables. Everyone got their assignments?" Miss Bessie asked.

"Yes, ma'am," we said, and everyone got to work. It was exciting because none of us had ever been in the kitchen of a restaurant, except Julie.

Miss Bessie turned the radio on as we worked, and we spent the next hour working and singing along to Madonna, Michael Jackson, and Prince. Sure that we understood our jobs, Miss Bessie retreated to the kitchen to run the dishwasher and put the kitchen and clean the kitchen.

Everything back in order there, she came to inspect our work out front.

"I think all of y'all need to come to work for me! This place has never been put back together so fast."

We beamed with pride. It wasn't often that Miss Bessie complimented anyone, let alone kids who were always making messes in her diner.

"Miss Bessie," I said.

"What, Carrie?"

"Um, what about the letter?"

Miss Bessie sighed. "What about the letter?"

"Who would write something mean like that?" I asked.

"Well, it seems like it could be anyone. The letters are all the town has talked about. This one was mean, but there are people in this town, as I am sure you've noticed, who hold grudges and find delight in the misfortune of others."

"You sound like Brother Bob," Emily said.

"Yeah, I guess I do. You want a Bible verse too?" Miss Bessie laughed.

"I've learned my lesson," Miss Bessie continued. "I thought the letters were funny, and the people deserved them. Until today. I guess I shouldn't have been so happy with them. Kids, you are never too old to learn new things about yourself."

"Well, is it true?" I asked.

"Oh, the cinnamon roll thing?" Miss Bessie asked.

I nodded, not wanting to hurt Miss Bessie any more than she already had been, but this was our first time to talk to someone who had been the subject of an *As Always* letter, and I didn't want to let it go. I looked at Emily and Julie for support. They gave a slight nod. We all wanted to know.

"Some of it is and some of it isn't," Miss Bessie said.

We waited, quiet.

"I have an award-winning recipe. It was my grandma's, and Julia has been trying to get it since she was a kid. But it's also true that I have used canned cinnamon rolls from time to time as a base when I was missing ingredients or in a crunch and didn't have time for the dough to rise. Lately, because there has been so much business, from these damn letters, I've been relying on it more and more. But I promise you I've never used those in any of the bake-offs."

"So technically, what you usually serve *is* the award-winning recipe," I said.

"Yes."

"Miss Bessie, why do you think someone is writing the letters?" Emily asked.

"I don't know. I've heard all the gossip and agreed that most of the theories were probably spot-on. Well, except that I wrote them to bring business in," Miss Bessie said.

I sucked in my breath sharp.

"Oh, relax, Carrie. Everyone in town knows y'all have been playing Hardy Boys, trying to crack the case." Miss Bessie laughed. "You haven't been subtle. Mary Lou told me you were there when Ms. Randall was getting her hair cut and you asked Mary Lou who she thought wrote the letters."

"Oh," I said. It disappointed me that my spy career ended before it really got started.

"And Mr. Williams said that he saw Kevin eavesdropping in the backyard. But, this is the most exciting thing to happen in Paradise Point in a long time. It's no wonder it's taking up all your free time."

"Miss Bessie, I'm sorry we thought it was you," I blurted. I couldn't contain my guilty conscience.

"Don't worry about it. This'll all pass, and things'll go back to normal and someone else will do something and the gossip mill will start again. Besides, it was an excellent theory. The diner has never been this full. Every day, all day and especially on Saturday, I can barely keep up—hence, the canned cinnamon rolls."

Miss Bessie moved toward the door, resting one hand on the push bar and the other on the lock. "I think you've spent enough time on this. Thanks for helping me clean up." The lock clicked, and she swung open the door. The bells jingled, and she said, "Now, go have fun the rest of the day."

"Wait. Miss Bessie, do you think Bradley wrote the letters?" Derrick asked.

"No. Why would you ask that?" she answered.

"Because we saw him slide an envelope under the front door of the newspaper office and when we looked in the window, it was addressed to the editor of the *Paradise Point Gazette*, in his handwriting," Emily said.

"Well, now. That is an interesting development."

Chapter 18

"Back to the beginning," Emily said, taking over the conversation.

We sat at a picnic table in the park. The one farthest from the playground and the bathrooms. Even if every grown-up in town knew we were trying to figure this out, it was thrilling to keep up the secrecy. And we didn't want anyone else to get credit for all our hard work. It only occurs to me now that no one really cared about what we thought as kids.

"Okay, the first letter was about Mrs. Johnson letting Chester poop in Mrs. Stewart's yard," Emily said.

"And don't forget, letting him eat the flowers," Brian added.

"Let the record show that Brian remembered the detail about the flowers." Emily rolled her eyes.

"What record?" Brian asked.

"Never mind," Emily said.

"And remember? Miss Bessie thought it was hilarious, especially how mad Mr. Johnson got," Julie said.

"Yeah, but that doesn't mean she wrote it," Kevin said.

"Okay, moving on. The second letter was about Miss Mary Lou and the head lice," I said.

"Yes, but no one got head lice who had appointments that week. And Carrie said neither Miss Mary Lou nor Ms. Randall were itching their heads," Julie said.

"Except Bradley said Coach Thompson's wife had lice, and Mr. Williams said someone bought all the lice shampoo," Charlie said.

"Yeah, and we know that Miss Mary Lou and Mrs. Johnson had some kind of fight all this time. But Miss Mary Lou wouldn't have written a letter about herself. She lost too much business, and was pissed at whoever did," Kevin said.

"Moving on. The third letter was about Mrs. Jackson and Mr. Bennet. Miss Mary Lou isn't a fan of Mrs. Jackson, but she also didn't mention her name when she was yelling at Mr. Williams, did she?" Emily asked Kevin.

"No. I don't think so. She yelled about a lot of other ladies, though," Kevin confirmed.

"All right. The next letter was about Miss Bessie, and, like Miss Mary Lou, she knows everything about everyone. That's one reason it could be one of them writing the letters," Emily said.

"But there's no way it was Miss Bessie," Charlie said.

"Unless... What if there's more than one person writing the letters?" I said. "Think about it. Ms. Randall just types in the letters in the newspaper. We don't have handwriting to compare. It could be more than one person, and we'd never know."

"But Bradley might. He's always at the newspaper, pestering Ms. Randall to let him help. And he was there the day they found the first letter," Derrick said.

"And he was the one who told us Coach Thompson's wife had head lice," Emily said.

"But why would he write a letter about his own mama?" I asked.

"Okay then, what about Ms. Randall? Carrie, you said when she was at Miss Mary Lou's shop, you heard Miss Mary Lou offer to help her, probably give her gossip for the paper. She knows everything about everyone, just like Miss Bessie," Charlie said.

"And Mr. and Mrs. Johnson were mad at Ms. Randall," Emily said.

"Yeah, and so were Miss Mary Lou and Mrs. Jackson," I said.

"Everyone was mad at her at the town meeting. Remember, she had to sneak out the back," Julie said.

"And you said that Ms. Randall said that they haven't had to collect any papers for recycling since the letters. Everyone wants one," Derrick said in my direction.

"But if she's writing the letters, then what's she going to do? Write letters about everyone in town? Eventually, she'll run out of stuff to write about and have to move to another newspaper," I said.

"And now we're back to Bradley," Emily said.

"And we've already decided Bradley wouldn't have written a letter about his mama," I said.

I wasn't sure why I was defending Bradley. But I was sure he was a mama's boy. There was no way he was going to do something that mean to her. It was a dead end.

"Look, Carrie, we can't rule anyone out, even boys you like," Emily said.

"I already told you, I don't have a crush on him! If he was writing any letters, I just wanted to make sure there weren't any about me." My voice shook, and I tried to get it back under control. I knew if I got too excited, Emily would keep teasing me.

"Okay, okay," Emily said. "Besides, I guess he isn't that bad if you like stuck-up weirdos."

I let the comment pass. It was never a good idea to argue with Emily. Besides, it didn't matter, anyway. Bradley wasn't the one writing the letters.

"If we're finished talking about Carrie's love life," Kevin said, as I gave him a hard nudge to the ribs. "Oww! Take it easy." He laughed. "As I was saying, I think we need to figure out why anyone would write the letters. Someone is always doing something irritating in Paradise Point. Why write about it now?"

It was unusual for the boys to have a well-thought-out plan. They were mostly good for pranks and making up new games and dangerous stunts. It was pretty impressive that Kevin was thinking in a way that even Emily hadn't.

"All right, Kevin," Emily said, "what are you thinking?"

"Money. All the grown-ups care about is money. Mostly how much they have or how much they need. Some people are making money from these letters."

"We've already talked about this. Ms. Randall is selling more papers than ever, and Miss Bessie's diner is full from open to close," Julie said.

"Yes, but what about Mr. Williams? The grocery store ran out of lice shampoo, and Miss Bessie was havin' to buy groceries from him between deliveries. He probably sells dog poop bags, too. And Ms. Randall doesn't own the paper. She's just the editor," Charlie said.

"Yeah, but Mr. Williams was angry that someone wrote such a mean letter about Miss Mary Lou," Kevin said.

"And who makes money from the letter about Mrs. Jackson and Mr. Bennet? And Miss Mary Lou is the only beauty shop in town. She doesn't have any competition. No one is trying to steal her business," I said.

We were back at square one. Something was missing. Some piece of the puzzle had yet to reveal itself, and we didn't know where to look.

"I still feel bad about Miss Bessie," I said.

"Yeah, of all the letters, that one was the meanest," Derrick said.

Chapter 19

"What are y'all doing?" Bradley asked.

"Jeez, Bradley! Announce yourself. Don't come creepin' around here," Julie said, nearly jumping out of her skin.

When our group broke up to go home after hanging out on the monkey bars, Julie and I headed to her dad's restaurant. Her mom packed up hamburgers, fries, and a Coke for each of us. The restaurant was full, so we put the burgers and fries in our backpacks, careful not to smash them, and expertly rode one-handed so our Cokes would be available for the occasional sip.

Hoping to attract tourists, the City Council placed benches along Main Street. They were usually empty because there weren't very many tourists in those days. We decided a stake-out was in order and set up on the bench facing the newspaper office, partially hidden by the artist guild's iron works and wind chime exhibit. From that vantage point, we could see most of Main Street: the diner and library, the Jiffy store, post office, and the newspaper office.

That's where Bradley found us.

"I wasn't creepin' around. But it looks like you are," Bradley said.

"Shhh. Be quiet and sit down." Julie scooted over so there was a place for him. I moved closer to Julie, and Bradley crowded in on the bench next to me.

"Want some?" I held out my fries.

Julie glared at me.

"Thanks." Bradley took a few, eating them neatly, one at a time. Not like the rest of us cramming two or three into our mouths and wiping our greasy fingers on our shorts.

"You got a napkin?" he asked.

Julie rolled her eyes and handed him one from her bag.

"If you're going to sit with us, you have to be quiet," Julie insisted.

"What exactly are you doing?" Bradley whispered. "Don't y'all usually hang out at the park or the pool?"

"If you must know, we are people watching. This is the best place to do it. We can see most of the street from here," Julie said.

"It's the middle of the day. In the summer. There aren't any people out," Bradley said.

"We're watching the newspaper office," I said.

Julie glared at me again.

"Why are you watching the newspaper office? Ms. Randall is the only one who goes in and out. You can't even see her from here," Bradley said.

"Okay, here's the deal. We are trying to figure out who wrote the letter and maybe even who the next letter is about." I ignored Julie's subtle attempts to get me to shut up. I knew the rest of them didn't want Bradley involved, but he was the closest we could get to Ms. Randall. We had seen him deliver something, addressed in his perfect handwriting, to the newspaper office.

"I don't think Ms. Randall knows who is writing the letters," Bradley said. "I already asked her."

This thought hadn't occurred to us. So, we weren't the only kids interested in the mystery of the As Always letters. Not only was Bradley not the author of the letters, he was trying to figure out who wrote them.

"What did she say?" Julie asked.

Bradley shrugged and reached for another French fry. "She said she didn't know," he answered.

"But you were there when she found the first letter, right?" Julie asked.

"Yeah, it was on the floor when we unlocked the door to get the papers to deliver. Someone had pushed it through the mail slot."

"What did it look like?" I asked.

"Umm, I don't know. An envelope?" he said.

"Was it addressed to anyone? Or, just blank?" Julie asked.

"They addressed it to the Editor of the *Paradise Point Gazette*."

Exactly like what we had seen on the envelope we watched him deliver was in exactly the same way he described finding the first letter with Ms. Randall.

"Do you think Ms. Randall is writing the letters?" I asked.

"No."

"But she is the one who's finding them, and they're selling papers," I said.

"Ms. Randall isn't writing the letters. She isn't like that," Bradley said.

"What do you mean, she isn't like that?" I asked.

"I mean, she isn't mean like that. Besides, she isn't a writer. She's an editor."

"That doesn't mean she can't write," Julie said, exasperated.

I figured Bradley had better give us some useful information soon, or she was going to kick him off our bench.

"Obviously she can write," he said. "She doesn't write like that. Ms. Randall only writes articles about things going on in town that people need to know about. You know, like fishing, and town meetings, and school stuff. Things that people might find interesting," Bradley said.

"Seems like plenty of people find the As Always letters interesting," I said.

"Why are you always hanging around the newspaper, anyway?" Julie asked.

"Ms. Randall is teaching me stuff about the newspaper," Bradley said.

Bradley and I both wanted to be writers when we grew up. Only, he was the one Ms. Randall was helping. Probably because his grandparents owned the paper.

"Lucky you," I said, a little more sarcastically than I intended.

Bradley looked shocked at my tone. "Well, she knows I want to be a writer someday and maybe even work for a newspaper."

I was jealous. It really wasn't fair. Bradley couldn't help who his family was. Even if they let their dog poop in people's yards and eat flowers right off the bushes.

"Carrie wants to be a writer, too. She's always writing stuff down in her notebook," Julie said, trying to cheer me up.

"I know," Bradley said. "Ms. Randall has some friends from college staying here this summer. In that cottage Mrs. Jackson rents out. They're writers. They let me show them some things I've written. Maybe she'd introduce you, too. You could show them some stories you've written. You know, maybe they could tell you what they think," Bradley said.

It was an intriguing proposition. I was excited and scared just thinking about it. I'd never met an actual writer, and Ms. Randall didn't count.

"Really? Do you think Ms. Randall would introduce me?" I asked.

"I tell you what. We won't worry about asking Ms. Randall. They get coffee every afternoon at the diner. Why don't you figure out a way to be there tomorrow and I'll also be there, and we can both talk to them," Bradley said.

"Wait, you know them well enough to introduce me like that?" I asked.

"Yeah, I've been doing things for them all summer. They like me," Bradley said.

"Doing what sort of things?" Julie asked, suspicious that outsider grown-ups would ask Bradley to be their errand boy.

"Getting groceries, delivering food, mailing stuff, and getting their mail at the post office. Those kinds of things. They get into the 'flow' and can't be bothered with stuff like that. So, I go by once a day and they have a list and money for me, or there isn't anything and I just go on with my day," Bradley explained.

I looked at Julie, and she shrugged. We both knew about stranger danger. I'd get in so much trouble if Mama found out I was meeting grown-ups she didn't know. But it was with Bradley, and at Miss Bessie's, and they were actual writers. The risk of getting caught was worth a summer of grounding.

"Okay," I said, "I'll see you tomorrow."

Chapter 20

Unlike most Sunday mornings, I bounced out of bed. Dressed and ready to go, I waited impatiently for my family.

It wasn't unusual for me to have a book and a notebook everywhere I went, but it would be unusual for me to have my backpack at church. There would be too many questions, and then I'd have to give too many fake answers. I didn't lie very well. It was risky enough without drawing additional attention to myself.

I looked at my bookshelf, wondering which book might make me look like an author. I had quite a collection already. They were my favorite things, and I dreamed of having a library that was floor to ceiling books with a ladder that I could slide to any section I wanted to explore. For now, the shelf over my dresser would have to do.

I thought I could get away with bringing *Harriet the Spy*, because it was on the summer reading list. Mama would hold on to it, of course. She wouldn't let me read other books during church, but I could have it before, and while I waited for them to quit visiting with everyone else.

"I see you're up early and ready to go." Dad poured another cup of coffee. "Something big happening today?"

Oh no, I thought, *I'm already busted, and I haven't done anything yet!*

"Did y'all get a lead on the letter writer?" Dad asked with a smile.

"Oh, well, maybe. We had an idea, but every time we think we figure it out, then that person has a letter written about them," I said.

"Well, it sure has captured the whole town's attention. This is the most exciting thing that's happened in Paradise Point in a very long time," Dad said.

"That's what everyone says."

"Be careful. It's one thing to observe, and another to get involved. Don't give anyone a reason to gossip about you," Dad said.

"I know. Dad, how did you know we were trying to figure it out?"

"Y'all aren't the only wannabe detectives in town, Carrie. Don't forget, this is Paradise Point. You can't get away with anything. Not for too long, anyway. Everyone may talk about the letters in the paper, but all eyes are still on y'all," Dad said.

Church was stuffier than usual. I sat next to Mama and dutifully handed over my book as the choir took their places at the front of the church, singing "This is the Day the Lord Hath Made." *This is the day,* I thought. *The day I get to meet an actual writer.*

Brother Bob made some announcements, and I began my usual counting ritual to pass the time. This morning, I looked around and counted the color of dresses I could see without turning my head to the side. One yellow, three green, two pink, and one red. Then it was the number of fans. Ten. The number of "amens" I heard. One from Brother Bob, three from behind me, four from the front over by the piano, and two from the front by the number sign. Mixing it up, I added the numbers on the sign to the left of the pulpit: Sunday School Attendance, fifty-seven. Hymns pages sixty-eight, one hundred twenty-three, seven, and two hundred fifty-six. Worship Attendance, seventy-two.

I had to do the math in my head. *Let's see, one hundred twenty-three and seven is one thirty, plus two fifty-six is three eighty. Okay, three eighty plus fifty-seven is... Oh wait, did I already add fifty-seven? I need my notebook.* I lost track of which numbers I had already added. Abandoning the math problem, I tried to guess which hymns we were going to sing, except I never paid much attention to the hymns, so I didn't recognize any of the page numbers. *Wait,* I thought, *I wonder why there are more people in church than Sunday school.* I didn't understand why. Especially considering you had snacks in Sunday school, and we couldn't eat or drink anything in church. If I had the choice, I'd pick Sunday school only.

With my counting and failed math problem abandoned, I looked at my watch, sure that church was about to be over. Nope. Still, almost an hour. Fidgeting while Brother Bob droned on, I looked over at Emily, and she shrugged. I carefully turned to see what Derrick was doing. He stuck his tongue out and crossed his eyes. I tried really hard not to, but the giggles came, and Mama made me turn around, just as I saw Bradley give a quick wave. That cured the giggles. I hoped Emily hadn't noticed.

"Scripture reminds us in 1 John 1:9, that 'If we confess our sins, he is faithful and just and will forgive us our sins and purify us from all unrighteousness.' Now, many of you know that for the fourth week in a row, they have made someone in our town the subject of gossip and rumor," Brother Bob said.

"It isn't rumor if it's true!" I heard someone say from the back of the sanctuary.

A round of laughter erupted around the room.

"That is enough and not the point, Mr. Atkins. And I'll kindly ask you not to interrupt my sermon again.

"Two of the fine ladies of our congregation have been the subject of these letters, and two of the businesses in our community have suffered great losses because of these personal attacks."

Brother Bob mopped his face and reached over the pulpit for a glass of water. It was hot in church that morning and about to get hotter.

"What has made these personal attacks even worse is the person writing them hasn't come forward, so there is no way for any of these women to confront them. God is concerned, and so am I, that so many of you are getting enjoyment from the suffering of others."

Here it comes. The going straight to Hell talk.

I looked over at Emily, and could tell she was waiting for it, too.

"As scripture says, it's important for whoever is doing this to come forward, ask forgiveness for the destruction she has caused, and repent."

Emily's frantic wave caught my eye. "She," she mouthed.

I shrugged, wondering if Brother Bob was preaching to one person in church that day.

"You know who you are," Brother Bob said. "As the choir sings hymn one fifty-eight, reminding us that only the blood of Jesus can wash away our sins, I'll be standing here waiting to pray with you."

The piano started, and we stood. Everyone's eyes trained on the front of the church, waiting to see who God was going to move to the front to take up Brother Bob's offer to pray for forgiveness and repent.

No one moved a muscle.

Chapter 21

We were quieter than usual, filing out of church. Brother Bob had moved to his usual place guarding the back door, so we had to shake his hand and tell him what a wonderful sermon it was before we were free to leave. The line moved quickly. No one wanted him to look too deeply in their eyes, lest he root out some gossipy sin and require them to confess and repent right there.

"Did you see her?" Emily asked, trying to get past me to the swing first.

"Who?"

"Ms. Randall. She snuck in the side door. Tripped over something as she was trying to find a seat."

"When did you see her?" I asked.

"I didn't. I heard Mrs. Jackson whisper something about it to Ms. Richardson. Mrs. Jackson is almost as deaf as Mr. Belton. She can't whisper. I tried to turn around, but Mama gave me the pinch. I had to sit still."

I looked over at the grown-ups milling about in their little groups, each faction trying their best to surreptitiously determine who Brother Bob was referencing without getting caught gossiping on church property. I wanted to move as far away from church as I could, in case lightning from Heaven took out the building and all the sinners on the grounds.

"Hey, since when are your parents friends with the Johnsons?" Emily pumped her legs and swung higher and higher.

"They aren't really," I answered and looked over to see my parents, to my horror, talking with Mr. and Mrs. Johnson and Bradley.

"Uh oh," I said, just as my dad caught my eye and waved me over.

"Hey, Carrie, come here," Dad called.

"I gotta go. I'll talk to you later," I said, rushing to get whatever was going to happen over with as quickly as possible.

I silently appealed to God to see all the gossip and meanness and send a lightning bolt to rescue me from whatever I was walking into. Surely, my parents knew about my plan and would ground me forever.

It was worse than I expected.

"Carrie, Mr. Johnson was telling me that some of Ms. Randall's friends are here writing for the summer. Did you know that?" Dad asked.

"Yes, sir," I said. He seemed excited, not mad. This was confusing.

"Well, he said Bradley has spent some time with them and they have even talked to him about writing. Read some things he's written and given him some pointers. Notes, I think they are called, right, Bradley?" Dad asked.

"Yes, sir. Notes," Bradley answered, nodding.

I stood there looking nervously at Bradley, wondering if he had something to do with this.

"I mentioned to Mr. Johnson here that you want to be an author, and he said that Bradley is going to visit with them this afternoon at the diner and asked if you wanted to go too. I didn't want to agree without talking to you first, but I think it would be a great opportunity. What do you think? You want to go?" Dad asked.

I could barely contain my excitement at being allowed to meet these strangers.

"Yes," I said, a little too loudly and quickly.

The breath Bradley had been holding in whooshed out in a sigh. He must have been as relieved as me.

"All right, let's get home and you can change. Bill, what time is Bradley going to the diner?" Dad asked.

"Two o'clock," Bradley said. "That's when they usually get there."

"Sounds good. That gives us time to get something to eat and you'll have plenty of time to ride your bike over there," Dad said.

The Johnsons turned to walk toward their house. It was only a couple of blocks from the church. We turned toward our house and from my side, I could see Emily and Derrick, standing at the swing, making faces and being dumb. But I didn't care. Let them be stupid. I had a feeling that although Bradley didn't write the letters, he may have a clue we needed. *And why was Ms. Randall suddenly at church this morning?* Maybe her writing friends would know.

I slid my bike into the rack at exactly 1:45 that afternoon. It was early, but Bradley had said that they get there around 2:00. I was nervous that Miss Bessie wouldn't be open after the fiasco yesterday. But as I had rounded the corner and raced down Main Street, I could see the neon Open sign and smelled the now infamous cinnamon rolls. I heard the bells jingle as customers walked from the air-conditioned diner into the humid afternoon.

Bradley looked up from where he sat and waved me over when the bells announced my arrival. Miss Bessie watched from behind the counter, looking at me over her round frames, smiling as if she were in on some secret.

"Hey, Carrie, I rarely see you in here on a Sunday afternoon. You joining Bradley?"

I looked at Bradley just now, realizing that he was sitting at a table alone.

"Um, yeah, I guess," I said.

"She's not joining me," Bradley said, a little too quickly. "We're just waiting for the writers. Ms. Randall said they'd be in this afternoon. You know, for coffee."

"Oh, yeah. I guess it is about that time." Miss Bessie checked the time on the clock hanging over the window in the kitchen. "They should be here any minute. Y'all want something while you wait?"

I thought about what a writer would have. Coffee seemed too grown-up, not to mention too hot for a summer afternoon.

"Can we have a Coke, Miss Bessie?" Bradley asked.

"Two Cokes coming right up," Miss Bessie said.

I approached the table and wasn't sure where to sit. *Was this like at church where everyone had an assigned seat? Would I make a writer mad if I sat in their place and then they wouldn't read my writing and I'd never get to be published?* I panicked, unsure what to do, when Bradley pushed the seat out next to him.

"You can sit here," he said. "Unless you'd rather sit somewhere else."

I was relieved not to have to decide and accepted his offer.

"This is great, thank you." I scraped my chair until it was under the table.

"Two Cokes on the house. Anything else?" Miss Bessie winked at me.

"Oh, I have money." I pulled some wadded bills from my shorts pocket.

Miss Bessie waved me off. "I'll want y'all's autograph when you're rich and famous."

Bradley and I laughed and ripped the top of the straw wrappers off and blew through them, sending the wrappers into each other's faces. We were still giggling when the bells above the door jingled and in walked the strangest people I'd ever met.

It surprised me to see a mix of five men and three women who seemed much younger than I had pictured. In my mind, writers were old, wore glasses and tweed coats, and spent their time hunched over typewriters, pecking away. These were young people—well, younger than my parents, which was the bar for being geriatric. And they were wearing shorts, or long flowy skirts, and flip-flops. The one consistency with my imagination was the glasses. Every one of them was wearing a pair, and one had a pair on his face and another perched on his head.

They laughed easily at some inside joke and seemed unaware of me and Bradley waiting for them.

"Good afternoon, Miss Bessie," the one in the flowy skirt said.

"Y'all go on and sit. I assume the usual, coffee and rolls?" Miss Bessie asked.

The man who seemed in charge of the group nodded and thanked her.

"Hey there, Bradley! Who's this?" The woman with unruly curly red hair sat across from him. She pushed her glasses up on her nose and leaned on the table with her elbows.

"Maggie, this is my friend Carrie," Bradley said.

"It's nice to meet you, Carrie," Maggie said. And then to the group, "So, this is the famous Carrie?"

Bradley blushed.

Bradley was right. Everyone adjusted to make room for me. It wasn't like church, like I was worried.

"Hey," I said.

Jeremy appeared with a tray full of plates, a platter of cinnamon rolls hot and gooey from the oven, a carafe of coffee, and eight cups.

"Bradley, how was it yesterday with the latest letter? Every week we try to make it to the diner, but you know we keep strange hours and usually we sleep until noon on Saturday. Carrie, Bradley has been telling us the craziest things about your little town. We've especially enjoyed hearing about these letters to the editor. What a quirky place," the blond man wearing a faded black T-shirt at the head of the table said as everyone began helping themselves to fresh coffee and cinnamon rolls.

"It's quite delightful," said the woman to my left. "We've never spent time like this in such an isolated place. It's healing for burnout, and when Lydia, I guess Ms. Randall to you, suggested we come for the summer, we all jumped at the chance."

"And it's helped all of us get out of our writing slumps," the man said, sitting directly across from me.

"Although, we really haven't seen Lydia as we'd hoped, have we?" the lady on Bradley's right said, twirling her long, dark ponytail.

"But anyway, go ahead, Bradley. Tell us about yesterday's letter," the ponytail lady said.

"It was something else. The town was in an uproar because Miss Bessie kicked everyone out and closed for the day." Bradley paused, taking a long drink from his frosty Coke. "But Carrie is always here. Carrie, what was it like?"

All heads turned in my direction.

"Oh, well." I looked nervously in Miss Bessie's direction. She focused on the receipts, so I leaned in close. "It was awful! Someone wrote that Miss Bessie, well, you know, her award-winning cinnamon rolls?"

Their heads nodded in unison. They were chewing on those award-winning rolls as I spoke.

"Someone wrote that they aren't an original recipe."

I sipped from my glass and swallowed before speaking again, lowering my voice even more than before. "They wrote she uses canned cinnamon rolls. You know, the ones from the grocery store."

"No, that can't be," the woman with the curly brown hair said, quickly taking a bite and glancing at the man at the head of the table. "These cinnamon rolls? The ones we are eating now?" She swallowed and then covered her mouth with the napkin.

"Yes," I answered.

"What happened then?" the young man across from me asked, and I swear he looked like he was smiling.

"Miss Bessie got mad, and she stormed over to take the paper from Mr. Lewis. But Mrs. Johnson got there first."

"Bradley, isn't your last name Johnson?" the man in charge asked.

"Yes."

"Any kin to that Mrs. Johnson?" the lady with the long, dark ponytail asked.

"That's my mama," Bradley answered. He seemed embarrassed about what was coming next.

"The one who didn't pick up the dog poop a few weeks ago?" the man across from us with the dark hair asked, taking a long sip from his coffee mug.

"Yes, the same one," Bradley answered.

"Okay, go on," the lady with the curly brown hair instructed.

"Oh, so Mrs. Johnson, Bradley's mama, got there first and yanked the paper from Mr. Lewis and pretended to give it to Miss Bessie and then yanked it away as Miss Bessie was reaching for it."

I hesitated, glancing toward the counter, but Miss Bessie had moved to the kitchen and was well out of earshot.

"And?" the lady with the ponytail asked, looking around the table. They smiled as if they shared some kind of secret.

"And Miss Bessie accidentally hit Mr. Lewis in the face when she reached for the paper. Then there was all this commotion, and Mr. Lewis knocked over a tray full of dishes."

I had them on the edge of their seats. My storytelling abilities captivated them, or so I thought. Taking a long swallow from my Coke, I glanced at Bradley.

"Mrs. Johnson, Bradley's mama, was weaving in and out, with Miss Bessie in hot pursuit, closing in, while Mrs. Johnson read the rest of the letter."

"What was in the rest of the letter?" the man at the head of the table asked.

"That Miss Bessie wouldn't give out the recipe, because she couldn't. She didn't have the recipe because they came from a can in the store. Oh, and that everyone has been overpaying for something they could make at home."

It was exhilarating to have a captive audience. I took another drink.

"Mrs. Johnson had a fit and said a cuss word, because she has been trying to get that recipe forever. Miss Bessie always said it was her grandmother's recipe, and Mrs. Johnson is Miss Bessie's cousin and thought she should have the recipe too," I said.

"Wow, sounds like quite a scene," the lady with the curly hair said, making some notes in her journal.

I had a flash of a memory. I couldn't quite place it, and something distracted me for just a second watching her write.

"It was. Miss Bessie got to the front and opened the door and told everyone to get out. She said a few cuss words too, but we weren't able to get out quick enough."

"Oh, why not?" the lady with the long, dark ponytail said.

"Business at the diner has been super busy since the letters. Everyone comes on Saturday to hear Mr. Lewis read the paper. He reads it like the guy at the circus. You know, the one in the middle who makes all the announcements?"

I had only been to the circus once, and I couldn't remember what that was called.

"The ringmaster?" Bradley offered.

"Yes, that's it. Mr. Lewis is like a ringmaster. You really should come this Saturday. No telling what will be in the paper after this letter."

"Anyway," I continued. "When we got there, Miss Bessie had us sit on the floor, over there." I pointed to the place where the counter and the dessert display case met.

"On the floor?"

"Yeah, it wasn't a big deal until Derrick got his fingers stepped on twice. But everything happened so fast that we couldn't get up and out with everyone else. We just sat there. I guess we planned to sneak out when Miss Bessie wasn't looking, but we didn't have the chance. She caught us when she started cleaning up."

"That must have been awkward," the man across from us said.

"It was. We just helped her get everything back in order," I explained.

"That sounds like an exciting morning for you and your friends," the man in charge said.

"Yeah, I guess so. All our Saturday mornings have been pretty exciting since the letters started. We spend all week trying to figure out who is writing them," I said.

"You should see them too," Bradley said. "Sneaking around town, listening to the grown-ups talk, trying to figure it out like they are detectives or something."

"Like Harriet the Spy?" the lady with the ponytail asked with a huge smile.

"Carrie carries a notebook and everything," Bradley said. "Go on, show them."

"So, have you figured out who is writing the letters?" the man in charge asked, also jotting a few things down in his journal.

"No." I rummaged around in my bag for my journal. Damn that Bradley. I wanted to choose what I was going to show them, if they asked to read something. Now I felt like I had to hand over my notebook with all my town notes in it. And Bradley might not be too happy with what they read.

I placed my hands firmly on top of my journal on the table in front of me.

"As soon as we think we know, then the letter is about that person. No one would write a nasty letter about themselves," I said. "So, we have to start over."

"Is that your notebook?" the lady with the brown curly hair asked.

"Yes."

"May I?" She reached for it.

I glanced nervously at Bradley before handing it over.

"Don't worry. Bradley shows us some of his notes, too. It's good that you keep a notebook. Every writer should have one, and something to write with, at all times. You never know when something right in front of you triggers an idea for a story."

She smiled, opening my notebook and, flipping through, read a passage here and there.

"Listen to this," she said.

I braced myself for whatever she was going to read.

"The diner was crazy this morning. Mr. Lewis read a letter that made Mr. Johnson so mad. They said Mrs. Johnson let Chester poop in Mrs. Stewart's yard and didn't pick it up. What's the big deal about dog poop? Just don't step in it. I guess she also let Chester eat some flowers, too. Wouldn't that make him throw up? Seems like that would be an appropriate punishment for Mrs. Johnson."

The lady with the curly hair laughed. "Good observation. I bet he puked his guts out." She flipped through a few pages.

"I wonder if anyone else noticed the benches by the art co-op. You can see everything and no one can see you, not unless they are right next to you, anyway. People don't pay attention. I saw a kid running with an ice cream cone trip, and the ice cream bounced right off the cone and into the street. It was hilarious!"

"I bet it was," the lady with the ponytail said. They all laughed, and I couldn't help but notice the feeling of pride, having captured something that others found funny, too.

The curly-headed lady flipped a few more pages.

"I wonder where Ms. Randall is getting the letters from. Everyone is blaming everyone else. All these grown-ups have so many connections from way back. I wonder if I will have connections like that if I live here forever, too."

The lady with the curly hair looked up. "Probably. Do you want to live here forever?"

"I don't know," I answered.

The guy in charge reached out for the notebook. "Let me have a look," he said, and she handed it over.

No one asked me.

He opened it to the middle and raised his eyebrows.

"It was hilarious. The whole town is going crazy because someone said that Miss Mary Lou was giving people head lice. I don't know why. Miss Mary Lou cut my hair last week, and I didn't get head lice and she didn't seem like she had an itchy head. Besides, Bradley said that Coach Thompson's wife bought all the lice shampoo. What does that have to do with Miss Mary Lou? I wonder how Bradley knows so much about it, anyway. He's always lurking around, watching everyone. Maybe he is the one who wrote the letter?"

"I did not," Bradley insisted, sitting up straighter in his chair.

The guy in charge smiled at the lady with the curly brown hair.

"I didn't say you did." I turned to face him. "I wrote, 'I wonder how Bradley knows so much about it.' I was just brainstorming. You know, thinking of all the possibilities."

It did not satisfy Bradley.

"You know what? All summer, you and your little group of friends have been trying to figure out who has been writing the letters. You have been the ones spying on everyone and writing everything down in your notebook. Maybe you wrote the letters," Bradley said.

This was not going the way I had hoped. When I agreed to come, I had envisioned being discovered. Having these writers see my talent and immediately I would write books and articles and be famous. Besides, I was the one defending him from the rest of our group.

I was about to tell him I had been his biggest defender when he said, "Don't forget I caught you and Julie the other day sitting on the bench where no one could see you, spying on the whole town. You want to be a writer, and suspiciously there hasn't been a letter about you or anyone in your family. I bet you are the one writing all the letters just to see your words in print."

That was it.

"Bradley, for your information, I have defended you every time your name has come up in our conversations. Emily and the others bring you up constantly, but I said, 'No, Bradley isn't like that. Besides, he wouldn't write something to embarrass and humiliate his own mama because he is too much of a mama's boy!'"

I had gone too far, and in front of grown-ups too.

"Besides, we saw you deliver something to the newspaper."

Bradley's eyes widened.

"Yep, you thought you were sneaking around, being so clever. But if you want to deliver something in secret, I suggest you not do it in the middle of the day," I said.

I sat back and faced the lady with the curly brown hair. The outburst was exhausting.

"See, I told you she sneaks around, spying on everyone in town. Her and her friends," Bradley said, a little more subdued.

The man in charge calmly closed my notebook and slid it back across the table. Judging by the look on his face, our argument amused him.

"You have the makings of a fine author, Carrie. I hope you continue noticing things and write them down. That is what all talented writers do. And that is what we have been encouraging Bradley to do all summer as well. If you want to be a writer, you just have to write all the time about everything you see that is interesting to you. But you don't have to show it to everyone," he cautioned. "Bradley, it seems she isn't the only one who, how did you put it?"

The man looked at the curly-headed lady and she read from her notebook, "Spies on the whole town, is what I heard. Same?" She looked at the lady with the long, dark ponytail.

"Yep, that's what I wrote, too," she said.

I looked at Bradley, and our eyes locked. Neither of us had noticed them taking notes during our heated exchange. *What did this mean?*

"All of this can be very helpful when you are documenting things, or useful to develop characters and dialogue for a story. You are well on your way, both of you, to being talented writers."

My breath settled into a steady rhythm as I took it all in. Bradley sat back in his chair too and took a long sip from his Coke.

Miss Bessie interrupted the silence.

"Y'all need more coffee?" She picked up the pot and checked its contents.

"Sure," the man in charge answered. "And some more of those cinnamon rolls, too. I hear they are award-winning."

Miss Bessie leveled her stare at him. "Yes, they are. And you are in luck. I just took a batch from the oven. I'll bring them right out." She hesitated before returning to the kitchen.

"You know, y'all picked an exciting summer to spend writing in Paradise Point. Usually, nothing happens here. It's a pretty quiet community. But this summer, things are more exciting than usual. What with the letters in the paper, and all." Miss Bessie looked at the group of writers. She just stood there, and I wondered if she was waiting for a response.

"Lydia said we'd get plenty of work done this summer. And it is a quaint little town. Perfect for writers. No distractions. That is what she had said. But these letters have been quite entertaining. We don't take the paper ourselves. It would be a distraction. But between Bradley and Lydia, they have updated us each week," the man said.

Miss Bessie looked over at Bradley. "I bet you have. Well, I'll be right out with fresh coffee and cinnamon rolls," and she swished herself right to the kitchen.

Chapter 22

We left the diner when the writers lost interest in us. I was confused. At first, they had seemed interested in my notebook, and they had encouraged me to continue writing everything I saw. But then they seemed more amused by the argument I had with Bradley than concerned about my being a famous writer one day.

The door closed behind us, and the bells were still jingling, announcing our departure, when we heard our names called from across the street. I looked up from the bike rack in time to see Emily and the others emerging from the same place Julie and I had been yesterday.

Bradley looked at me with a worried expression.

"What do they want?" he asked.

"Brace yourself," I answered with a sigh. I knew what was coming.

"Well, well, well, what do we have here?" Emily crossed her arms as she approached the bike rack.

"Hey. What are y'all doing?" I asked, hoping I sounded excited to see them.

"Just checking out your people watching bench. You can see so many people doing a lot of things from there. You're right. It's a brilliant spot. You can see the entire street." Emily swept her arms open for dramatic effect.

"I know. That's why I like it," I said.

"What was going on at the diner?" Kevin asked, eyeing Bradley with suspicion. "You usually have to spend Sundays with your family. Isn't that what you always tell us?"

"Yeah, usually I do. Today I didn't." I wanted to get away from them. I already had a big argument in public with Bradley. I didn't want to have one with Emily and everyone else. Mostly, I just wanted to go home and think about what happened in the diner. Something seemed off about the whole thing.

"Since when do you hang out with Bradley?" Emily asked.

I looked at Julie for some kind of support. She shrugged.

"Carrie wasn't hanging out with me," Bradley said.

Emily turned her attention to Bradley. "Oh really? I saw you get to the diner. Then we watched Carrie arrive. And you left at the same time. Seems like you were there together."

"Okay, Sherlock Holmes, your powers of deduction need some practice. We were in the same place in a small town. And believe me, we might not be again." Bradley pulled his red bike from the rack.

My glance bounced between Emily and Bradley. This was ridiculous.

"Wait a minute. Not that it is any of your business, Emily, but we were together in the diner. You caught us. We are in love, and I'm sure that we will grow up and get married and move far, far away from here," I said.

Emily stood still, apparently shocked at what I just said.

"Yeah, and when we're famous writers, we'll create horrible characters just like you," Bradley said, emboldened.

"What the hell?" Charlie asked, standing there like an idiot.

We continued the ruse.

"Yes, and when we are famous writers, we'll talk about the tiny town we grew up in and all the weird friends we used to have," I said.

"And when they make a movie about us and we have to do interviews with the movie stars, we'll mention that if it wasn't for this horrible girl named Emily, who constantly accused us of having crushes on each other, we'd never have realized that we were soulmates." Bradley grinned.

Emily said something, but Julie's infectious laughter drowned her words. The tension broke with the absurdity of our improvisation.

"What do you think now, Emily?" Charlie asked.

"I think you're all a bunch of idiots," Emily said.

She had loosened up but was still fuming underneath. I'd known her long enough to know that she didn't like being made to look like a fool, or have her authority questioned in our group. But I'd had enough conflict for one day.

"Wait, so are you really getting married?" Brian asked.

"Jeez, are you serious? We're twelve!" I said, exasperated.

This made Julie laugh even harder, and the Coke she had been sipping on sprayed from her mouth and nose on to the sidewalk. "Stop! I can't stand it anymore," she said, trying to catch her breath.

"Where are y'all goin', anyway?" I asked.

"To play *Pac-Man*. Derrick thinks he can knock off my high score. Want to come?" Julie asked.

I took a quick look at my watch. There was still time before Dad told me I had to be home. I looked at Bradley, unsure what to do. It seemed mean not to invite him, since he had invited me to meet the authors. But it might be even more mean to make him endure more time with Emily.

There was a moment of uncomfortable silence. Bradley was going to leave, and I wasn't sure what to do.

"Bradley, you can come too," Julie said.

Bradley looked to me, and I nodded.

"Yeah, come on. It'll be fun. Derrick thinks he's the best player, but mostly he's lucky. And he has more quarters than the rest of us, so he gets to play more often," I said.

"You sure?" Bradley asked quietly, nodding toward Emily.

"Totally. Come on." I got on my bike to ride down the street.

Chapter 23

The Jiffy store was quiet and cool on Sunday afternoons. People in Paradise Point used Sundays as lazy days, recovering from the week before and preparing for the week ahead. This was before the time of frenetic activity, round-the-clock cable news, and the schedules that put people in early graves. It was before tourists learned about our "quaint and quirky town" as the writers had called it, and changed everything. We had the place to ourselves, and it was glorious.

"Hey! Y'all keep it down," Ms. Richardson said from behind the counter. She was doing inventory, with boxes of merchandise strewn all around the front of the store. "I'm trying to count and y'all yellin' your high score numbers is messing me up!"

"Yes, ma'am," we mumbled, trying to be quiet. The competition was fierce. Julie and Derrick were playing two players to determine once and for all who was the best *Pac-Man* player in Paradise Point.

Usually, Ms. Richardson didn't care how long we played, as long as we didn't make too much noise and we bought plenty of Cokes and snacks. While we always found quarters for *Pac-Man*, we rarely had extra money for Cokes and snacks. Today we had enough for both.

I was sipping on my Coke and cherry Icee when Bradley approached from the chip aisle.

"Want some?" he offered, holding out his open bag.

I took a few, wondering how I would get the cheese dust off my fingers before it was my turn to play.

"Here." He handed me a napkin. "No one wants you to lick your fingers and then play."

"Thanks." I accepted the napkin and wiped my fingers before shoving it in my pocket. "So, about the diner," I said. "I'm sorry about all of that."

"About what?" he asked.

"You know. About my notebook and wondering if you were the one writing the letters. They only read snippets of what I wrote. It was out of context," I explained.

"I know," he said. "It doesn't matter. I know I didn't write them."

"And I'm sorry about the mama's boy comment. It was just what was in my head. I don't really think that."

I'd never really talked to Bradley other than when I had to at school or at church. But now, I was seeing something different. He had tried to be a part of our group. And he had gotten me the introduction with the writers. He was weird, but we were all weird. We were twelve.

"Bradley, who do you think is writing the letters?" I asked.

He looked at me, seeming to consider something. "I'm not sure. But every time I think I know, it turns out I'm wrong."

The whooping and hollering from Julie interrupted our conversation.

"Bam, that's it, Derrick, you big loser! It's over and I won! How's that for a high score?" Julie demanded, hands up, backing away from the video game.

"What the hell?" Derrick asked, incredulous. But then, with a sly smile, he said, "Best two out of three?" holding out more quarters.

"Let's go!" she said and the rest of us sighed, knowing it would be a while before we got another turn.

Chapter 24

We spent the rest of the day locked into an epic battle to the death, with Derrick ultimately coming out the victor in the *Pac-Man* duel. As far as I know, no one ever beat his high score as long as the machine was at the Jiffy store. Which was a very long time.

The week flew by. We had our usual jobs, but Fourth of July week was always special in Paradise Point. The town essentially shut down to prepare for the festivities.

The City Council brought in a small fair with a couple of rides and lots of games. Area restaurants set up booths for the food. There were shrimp peeling contests and face painting. The fire truck led the parade through Main Street, all the way to the park. Mr. Johnson dressed up like Uncle Sam for his grand marshal duties.

Residents from all over the county came to celebrate and enjoy a day of beaches and fun. There would be more people in Paradise Point than at any other time of the year. It was a big deal, and we couldn't wait.

We had agreed to meet at the lemonade stand and make a game plan. There was nothing better than the lemonade on the 4th of July in Paradise Point. I planned to have plenty of it.

"Where's Julie?" Derrick asked when I approached the lemonade stand.

"Probably at the Jiffy store practicing to kick your ass at *Pac-Man*," Kevin said.

I laughed. It would have been a good plan, but no one would skip the parade for anything, not even uninterrupted access to *Pac-Man*.

"She's helping her parents set up. We'll meet her in front of the post office," I said.

We had plenty of practice finding the perfect place to watch the parade. The shade at this time of day was best at the post office. Thanks to the city's efforts with the bench project, there were three long benches in a row under the awning that covered the sidewalk.

"Let's get our lemonade and get down there before anyone gets our spot." Emily checked her watch.

With frosty cups of lemonade sweating in our hot little hands, we made our way down Main Street toward the post office. It was right next to the newspaper office, and, for a moment, I wondered if Ms. Randall was working, or if she and her friends were enjoying the festivities.

"What the hell? Someone already got our bench," Emily said, as we got closer.

"Hey, I saved your bench for you," Bradley said, obviously proud of his efforts.

"Thank you." I nudged Emily, hoping she'd shut up and not be mean again. "That was nice. Wasn't it, Emily?"

Emily stood straight, eyes focused on Bradley. "Yes, very nice. Thank you. Although everyone in town knows these are our benches."

"Yes, everyone except any out-of-town visitors, and Ms. Randall said that because of the letters, they are expecting a larger group of out-of-towners than usual. I thought I'd get here first and save them. Oh, and I brought these," Bradley said, as we all settled onto the benches.

I sat next to him on the bench, and he pulled out a paper grocery sack with grease spots all over the bottom.

"Carrie, can you help me?" he asked.

"Sure. What is that?" I asked as he opened the bag. A strong fragrance of fried sugar and flour wafted like a cloud from the bag.

"Funnel cakes." He handed me the first paper plate with a funnel cake so big that the edge draped over the side. Most of us had never traveled to events outside of Paradise Point, so this was our first funnel cake experience.

"Pass it down," he instructed.

I did as I was told, resisting the urge to lick my fingers between passes. Julie arrived just in time, and because she was sitting on the end, she got the first taste.

"Mmm, this is amazing." She licked the sugar and grease off her fingers.

"Where did you get these?" Emily asked, with her mouth full and powder sugar puffing out of her mouth as she spoke. "They're delicious!"

Bradley beamed and handed me the last two plates, one for him and one for me. I held them, jealous that everyone else had already started devouring their fried sugary treat. He took a stack of napkins out and, placing them in his lap, crumpled up the bag and placed it in the trash bin in front of the newspaper office.

"My dad sponsored a funnel cake booth this year. They came in from out of state. He said they used to make them all the time when he was a kid."

He settled in next to me, and I handed him a plate. My free hand reached over and pinched off a piece of the hot greasy goodness. It melted in my mouth and was the best thing I had ever tasted. Even better than Miss Bessie's cinnamon rolls.

We sat quietly eating. Emily seemed to appreciate Bradley. At least while she was stuffing her face.

The parade was the usual. Different businesses in town sponsored floats, which were actually just decorated trailers pulled by trucks. There were a few beauty queens who had won contests throughout the county. I always thought that was stupid. *Why get dressed up and sit in the back of a convertible, sweating to death?*

"Look at her sweating to death." Julie pointed to this year's Miss Shrimp Festival riding in the back of a red convertible.

"Yeah, she's gonna look like Miss Heat and Humidity by the end of the parade," Derrick said.

There was the trailer with the baseball and softball team, both of which had done well in their summer leagues.

A few artists made a cool paper mâché scene full of giant fish on a trailer decorated with blue streamers to look like water and waves.

The best trailer was the City Council float. It was also the last and signaled the end of the parade.

"Look," Brian yelled, pointing in the distance.

The crowd went wild as the float rounded the corner.

This year's theme was the Summer Olympics, and each member wore red, white, and blue athletic attire. One member proudly held a fake torch with yellow, orange, and red streamers on the top.

We followed the end of the parade to the park, ready to join the festivities, sure it would be a day to remember.

The day did not disappoint.

Chapter 25

The crowd moved down the street, children dashing from side to side, excited to pick up discarded candy. We didn't have any time for that. Full from Bradley's funnel cakes, we didn't have any room for candy. It was time to celebrate.

Carnival games lined the pathway through the park, and we hesitated, unsure where to begin. The sugar high kicked in and we were ready for a day of fun competition that didn't include a video game.

"I guess let's just start here." Kevin stood in front of the balloon popping game. We handed the teenager manning the booth a quarter each, and he gave us three darts each in return.

"Ready, aim, throw!" Julie yelled.

Our darts flew, causing the teenager to jump out of the way of our assault.

"Hey! One at a time!" he yelled. "Or you have to leave."

We looked at him, astonished. We'd never had a teenager yell at us, and we weren't sure if we'd really get in trouble.

I looked at Kevin and Charlie, and they shrugged.

"Who is red?" Derrick asked.

Bradley held up his darts. "I am."

Derrick nodded toward the board with the multicolored balloons. A red dart had popped one balloon.

"Okay then." Derrick said, and turned back to the board. "Finish your turn."

"Wait," the teenager yelled as he stepped in front of the board and pulled all the other colors, putting them in their correct bin.

Bradley drew back and popped balloons with every dart.

"Good job. What do you want?" The teenager motioned toward the prizes on the shelf under the board.

"Umm, that." He pointed to the biggest squirt gun we had ever seen.

153

"Here you go." The teenager pulled it off the shelf and handed it to a beaming Bradley.

"I want one of those. I bet it works better than the other ones we have," Kevin said.

"But not better than the hose at Carrie's house." Derrick laughed.

We took turns with the rest of our darts. Bradley was the only one who got a prize. Winning earned him respect with the boys in the group. I hoped they would stop being weird about him hanging out with us. I shouldn't have worried. By the end of the day, they fully accepted Bradley into our group.

The games seemed to go forever, and we occasionally had to find a parent for more quarters. Thankfully, all our parents were involved in some capacity, so we could always find one with change to spare.

We ate and played our way through the afternoon and by the time the sun was setting, we'd had our fill of hot dogs, funnel cakes, and lemonade.

"Let's find our place on the beach. Especially since we don't have Bradley saving a place for us," Emily said.

I looked at her, and she smiled.

Emily's mama had a quilt ready for us, the same one we used at the picnic. We grabbed it from the historical society booth, made a stop at the ice cream cart, and found our places just as the sun dipped below the horizon.

Sunburnt and content, we waited with the rest of Paradise Point for the national anthem and Pledge of Allegiance. A fishing boat appeared offshore with a raised American flag and we got to our feet.

Over a loudspeaker, Mr. Johnson welcomed the crowd, residents and visitors, to the Paradise Point Fourth of July Celebration.

"It is with great joy we welcome you to our community. For our last celebration of the day, we'd like to turn your attention to the water for our fireworks display."

This was always the best part. A perfect ending to a perfect day. I scanned the beach. Families sat on blankets. There was barely any empty ground to see.

"Hey, look." I nudged Bradley. "Over there."

He looked in the direction I pointed and squinted in the low light of the streetlights.

"What?" he asked.

"Isn't that Ms. Randall with the writers?"

"Yeah. I think it is." He moved his head forward, trying to get a better look.

They sat at the picnic table by the monkey bars. That's when it hit me. I had seen them before. Sitting right at that picnic table the night of the town hall meeting. They were sitting there talking and writing in their notebooks, just like they were tonight. I wondered how they could see to write.

"What do you think they are writing?" I asked.

"I don't know. Maybe just some notes for their books," he said.

"They were sitting at that table, just like that, the night of the town hall meeting. Do you think they were writing about it?"

"I don't know. Maybe," he said.

"Or—oh no! They were right by us. What if they were writing about us?" I asked, a little creeped out.

"Why? Were y'all doing anything interesting?" Bradley asked.

"Just trying to figure out who wrote the letter that week. Oh, and listening and commenting on what was going on in the meeting," I said.

"Were they there for the big blow-up at the end?" Bradley asked.

"Yeah, that's when I noticed them writing," I answered.

"I don't know. They didn't mention anything to me," he said.

The night sky exploded with bright hues of red, white, and blue. It was impressive. Of all the things that Paradise Point offered, the Fourth of July fireworks were the best.

I looked over again at the writers and wondered what they could write about that was so important they weren't paying attention to the show.

The commotion started just as the last pop of fireworks lit the sky over Paradise Point. Right on the edge of the beach at the park, I heard loud voices. Women's voices.

I nudged Julie and nodded in that direction. "What's going on over there?"

"I don't know. Wait." She squinted, straining her head forward. "Bradley, is that your mama?"

Bradley scooted over to Julie's side on the quilt and looked where Julie had pointed.

"Yeah, I think it is," he said.

By now, the crowd was noticing the heated exchange at the edge of the park.

"Hey, Bradley, isn't that your mama?" Brian pointed toward the yelling ladies.

"Welcome to the party, Brian." Emily rolled her eyes. She must have noticed them and heard Julie ask Bradley to confirm it was, in fact, his mama.

"That's Miss Mary Lou with her," said Kevin.

"And Mrs. Jackson," Derrick said.

We were all scooting to the edge of the blanket to get a better look. Some grown-ups near them backed away, while others moved in closer for a better view. It looked like the fireworks weren't the only excitement in Paradise Point that night.

I looked over at the writers when I heard Miss Bessie's voice mingling with the other ladies. *It's all the ladies from the As Always letters.*

The ladies looked ready for a battle. The fireworks lit up the park as they moved with determination through the crowd. At first, I wasn't sure where they were heading and worried as they walked toward us. I racked my brain for anything we could have done.

"Where are they going?" Kevin asked.

"And why are they all together?" Julie asked.

It was a mystery. Most of them didn't like each other and had long-standing grudges that were well-documented in town lore.

"Bradley, they're headed to the writers' table." I pointed toward the table.

They had shifted their direction at the bank of extra trash cans the City Council had set out for the celebration.

"Lydia Randall," Miss Mary Lou said, approaching the table.

Ms. Randall looked up, and the writers scooted down the benches.

I wondered if they were as afraid of these women as we were.

"We'd like a word with you."

"This hardly seems like the time or place," Ms. Randall said. She looked confident, like she was ready to take them on.

"It's like challenging her to a duel," Charlie said.

I didn't think they would kill anyone.

"What gives you the right to come into our town and ruin our lives? Writing these insulting letters and printing them as if they are anonymous. To sell those fish wrappers?" Miss Bessie asked.

"You are an outsider. We welcomed you into Paradise Point, and this is how you repay us?" Mrs. Jackson asked. She looked out of place, dressed in a sundress and sandals in contrast to everyone else's shorts and flip-flops.

"Not to mention the businesses you have ruined," Miss Bessie said, as she and Miss Mary Lou took a step forward.

"That head lice letter cost me two weeks of customers," Miss Mary Lou said.

"And the reputations you have damaged, insinuating inappropriate relationships," Mrs. Johnson added. "You should be ashamed of yourself."

"Are you finished?" Ms. Randall asked.

The ladies stood there.

"Julia, I thought you'd be happy that something exciting finally happened in this sleepy little town. Your kid certainly is," Ms. Randall said.

My head snapped around to look at Bradley. His face reflected the shock I was feeling.

"What?" I asked.

Bradley shrugged.

"At least, that's what Bradley told us. Nothing ever happens here. And the kids finally have something fun to do this summer."

"Do not bring my son and his friends into this." Mrs. Johnson took a step closer to the table. "And do not print any more of those damn letters."

Ms. Randall stood up.

"Are they gonna fight?" Kevin asked.

Bradley shook his head. "I hope not."

"I hope so," Emily said, rising to her knees to get a better view.

"I will do what I want, and I will print what I want. And you can't do anything about it," Ms. Randall said.

And with that, Mrs. Johnson slapped Ms. Randall right across the face. It was the most spectacular Fourth of July Paradise Point had ever celebrated.

Chapter 26

All anyone could talk about the next day was the slap heard around the town. It was shocking. We'd seen grown-ups argue at town meetings, especially this summer, but we'd never seen them strike each other.

We gathered at the diner early Saturday morning. Bradley was the first to arrive, with his bike already in the rack. He was now an official part of our group.

He stood next to the door, a stack of newspapers at his feet, when I pulled up and put my bike in the rack next to his.

"How are you?" I asked. We hadn't spoken since he jumped up from the quilt to run to his mama and lead her away from Ms. Randall on the Fourth of July.

"Okay," he said. "My parents are really mad at Ms. Randall. Ms. Randall is really mad at my parents. And my grandparents are thinking of shutting the paper down while they decide what to do."

"Won't she get in trouble for slapping Ms. Randall?"

"No. My dad's the mayor," he said. "It's embarrassing. I got to the newspaper office early this morning, and Ms. Randall had the papers outside labeled for delivery, but she wasn't there. I delivered them and figured I'd end here instead of starting here. It's okay, isn't it?" he asked.

"Sure. You can sit with us," I said.

Kevin, Charlie, and Derrick pulled up just as we were about to walk in.

"Hey, your mama's something! The way she slapped Ms. Randall, that was awesome!" Kevin said, laughing.

"Yeah, it was all my parents talked about," Derrick agreed.

"It was the most exciting part of the Fourth of July fireworks," Charlie added.

Bradley stood against the door, holding it open so we could pass. All in, he placed the newspapers on the rack, snapping the wire lock in place.

Emily rushed in and pushed him over, nearly squishing Charlie right into the wall of the booth. "So how much trouble did your mama get into?" she asked.

"Not much," Bradley said.

I looked at him, and he looked down at the menu. I guess I wouldn't want all that attention if my mama did something crazy like slap another grown-up either.

The bells over the door announced Julie as she ran to the table.

"Is there another letter? I woke up late and thought I missed it!"

"Not so far," I said. "Mr. Lewis isn't even here yet."

I nodded to the table that usually sat Mr. Lewis, Mr. Carter, and Mr. Johnson.

"Bradley, is your dad coming to the diner today?" Kevin asked.

"I don't know. Things are pretty tense. To be honest, I'm surprised they let me come. My grandpa said I had to do my regular job, and I had nothing to do with this," Bradley said.

"But, Ms. Randall said you did," Emily said. "I remember, she said, and I quote, 'At least that's what Bradley told us. Nothing ever happens here. And the kids finally have something fun to do this summer.' Isn't that right?" Emily asked.

"I know she said that, but I don't know what she's talking about. I didn't write those letters, and I didn't tell Ms. Randall to, either. I wish she'd have just left me out of it," Bradley said.

Miss Bessie swished over. "I see y'all are here bright and early. Bradley, it's nice to see you here this morning. Will this be a regular Saturday morning thing?"

"Yeah, he's with us," Charlie said, and Bradley beamed.

"So, chocolate milk and my award-winning cinnamon rolls for everyone?" Miss Bessie winked.

"Yes, ma'am," we answered.

"Coming right up."

"Okay, so it has to be Ms. Randall," Emily said once Miss Bessie was out of earshot.

"I agree," Kevin said. "I overheard Mr. Williams and Miss Mary Lou talking. She said that Miss Bessie and Mrs. Jackson couldn't believe your mama slapped Ms. Randall, but that Ms. Randall deserved it for spreading all these rumors."

"But how do they know it's her? Isn't that just gossip, like the letters?" I asked.

"Miss Mary Lou said that it had to be her. I guess she and Miss Bessie and Mrs. Johnson and Mrs. Jackson had some kind of secret meeting and they decided she was the one with the most to gain. No one else in Paradise Point would do anything so mean."

"Bradley, did you tell Ms. Randall all of that stuff? I know you lurk around town 'noticing things,'" Emily said. "It's okay if you did. It's made the summer fun."

"No, I didn't. Why would I say something about my mama?" he answered.

Miss Bessie arrived with our chocolate milk and cinnamon rolls. "It's going to be busy again today." Miss Bessie looked around. "Y'all can stay to eat, but then I'll need this booth, okay?"

"Yes, ma'am," we said, reaching for our glasses and plates.

Mr. Lewis arrived with Mr. Carter and Mr. Johnson in tow. The preacher table filled up next. Brother Bob stopped to say something to Mr. Johnson on the way to his usual table.

"Do you think Brother Bob will remind Mr. Johnson that his wife will probably go to Hell for slapping Ms. Randall?" Derrick asked. A swift kick under the table reminded him that Bradley was sitting with us. "Oh, I'm sorry, Bradley," he added.

"I don't think you go to Hell for slapping anyone anyway," Julie added.

I looked at Julie and thought, *How nice it must be to go to the Methodist church, where you don't have to be threatened with Hell every time you do something bad.*

"Don't worry about it. Derrick doesn't know anything about Hell anyway," Julie said.

"I'm not," Bradley said.

After his second cup of coffee, Mr. Lewis stood, put some coins in the paper rack, and took out a copy of the most recent *Paradise Point Gazette.*

As was his Saturday morning custom, he cleared his voice to get everyone's attention. This morning, it only took one time.

"Let's see what Ms. Randall has prepared for us today." He opened the paper and scanned each section. "Thankfully, she isn't here in case someone else wants to give her a pop in the face."

There was nervous laughter among the diners as all eyes focused on Mr. Johnson.

"There won't be any more of that, I can assure you," Mr. Johnson said and gave Bradley a smile. "Will there, Bradley?"

"No, sir," Bradley said.

"Well, not that she didn't deserve it, I guess," Mr. Lewis said. "If she is the one writing the letters.

"Okay, here we go. Looks like the fishing will be best off the south side of the point, nearest the old village pier, in the mornings this week." Mr. Lewis peered over the top of the paper. "Does anyone know where this information comes from? Every week, we learn about where the fishing is best, but how can we know that in advance?"

No one said anything.

"Very well. I guess those who need to know now have access to that information. Okay, the county is still working on the highway, no surprise there. The Fine Christian Ladies Association meeting will be at the Baptist Church this time. Brother Bob, I hope you have medics on hand. Could be a bloodbath with those ladies."

The diners giggled.

"That was unnecessary," Brother Bob said. "I am sure Mrs. Jackson will keep the meeting on track."

"It might be her who needs the protection." Mr. Lewis laughed.

"Moving on. The fire department, with the ladies of the historical society, will have a bar-b-cue and bake sale, with a silent auction, in two weeks. They are raising money for a new fire truck and improvements to the fire station. Y'all be sure to stop by and buy your tickets. You'll want them to come quickly if your place is burning down."

He licked his finger to get a better grip before turning to the next section. He looked around the diner.

I think he thought he was building anticipation, but mostly he was annoying us. Again, I don't know why it didn't occur to me to buy a paper and not wait for Mr. Lewis to read.

His brow wrinkled, and he turned the pages over. "That's strange." He flipped back through the paper.

"Come on. Quit stalling," Mr. Carter said.

"I'm not stalling. There isn't a letter to the editor this week," Mr. Lewis said.

"Give me that." Mr. Carter reached for the paper.

The diner was quiet as Mr. Carter inspected each page.

"He's right. Nothing here." Mr. Carter handed the newspaper back to Mr. Lewis.

We sat stunned, unsure of what to do next. *What did we do before the letters?*

The bells over the diner jingled as Ms. Randall walked in, holding an envelope in Bradley's handwriting. It was the one we saw him slide under the door a week ago.

"What are you doing here?" Miss Bessie asked. "Come for more trouble?"

"No, I have something to read this morning." She looked in Mr. Lewis's direction. "If you don't mind."

Mr. Lewis made a gesture, giving her the floor, and sat in his seat.

Ms. Randall nodded at him and held the paper up to read.

"Dear Lydia, thank you for telling us about this wonderful little piece of paradise. It was just what we needed. A place to get away and stoke our creativity to finish on deadline. The home you arranged was perfect for our needs and your assistant, Bradley, was very helpful so we could write uninterrupted by mundane tasks. He was funny, the way he talked about you and the town. We're sure by now you know it was us writing the letters as an exercise in creativity, a writing prompt of sorts. We would watch the town and each night report something interesting we had seen. Then choose the one we thought was the best and brainstorm a letter, type it, and one of us would drop it off, obviously undetected."

Ms. Randall took a breath and sighed.

"It was easy, overhearing conversations, seeing strange things in trash cans, observing people on our daily jogs, and noticing weird purchases in Mr. Williams's grocery store the times we ventured out for supplies on our own.

"You were wonderful! Reacting to the letters created all the chaos we needed to be inspired again about our characters and stories, and as a result, we finished our manuscripts, and they are already on their way to our publishers. We will give acknowledgment to this strange little town in all our books and hope that it will draw other writers to come for inspiration as well.

"Our parting advice to you is you should probably let go of some of the lingering grudges from the past. They aren't serving you well. The fascinating, unanticipated consequence was the town's unending desire to find out who was writing them and why. And of course, we did not know it would spark such animosity and raise old rivalries. It made our characters richer and much more interesting as we watched how you reacted. We hope you will forgive us for the trouble we caused. Please read this at the diner so they will know definitively it wasn't you.

"If we learned anything about Paradise Point, it's that gossip travels fast! Maybe next time, fill the newspaper with more interesting pieces of your own instead of depending on letters to the editor. As Always, Here to Make You Better."

She folded the letter.

"It seems my friends took advantage of all of us. And by the way, I do write all my own stories."

Don't miss out!

Visit the website below and you can sign up to receive emails whenever Brooke Baxter publishes a new book. There's no charge and no obligation.

https://books2read.com/r/B-A-KMLQ-VPCNC

BOOKS 2 READ

Connecting independent readers to independent writers.

Did you love *As Always*? Then you should read *The Santa Scoop*[1] by Brooke Baxter!

[2]

Memorial Summit Mall might not have a Santa this Christmas and journalist Sam Sanders is reluctantly investigating. Richard, her Christmas obsessed editor, assigned the story and she really needs to keep this job. As one interview leads to another, Sam gets closer to the true identity of Santa Claus and proof he actually exists. An anonymous letter, an invitation to a secret Santa association, and an unlikely friendship with the big man himself, lead Sam on a wild Christmas adventure that ends with an interesting alliance that just might save the Memorial Summit Mall Santa, and mall Santas everywhere.

---

1. https://books2read.com/u/3J6VKJ

2. https://books2read.com/u/3J6VKJ

Also by Brooke Baxter

A Paradise Point Novel
As Always

Standalone
Christmas Girl
The Santa Scoop

About the Author

Brooke Baxter, voracious reader, always wanted to be a writer. Her first two novels, Christmas Girl, a Carolyn Reader's Choice Award Finalist, and The Santa Scoop, combined her love of rom-coms and cozy mysteries to explore the magic of Santa Claus.

Brooke loves following quirky characters, as they navigate the most absurd circumstances. Her new book, As Always A Paradise Point Novel, explores the shenanigans of a small coastal town through the eyes of one of its younger inhabitants, a twelve-year-old girl.

She lives in South Texas with her husband. Brooke loves to hear from fans of her books at brookebaxterbooks@gmail.com. You can follow her on Goodreads and Facebook to get to know her better and to find out about new releases.

Read more at https://www.facebook.com/brookebaxterbooks.

www.ingramcontent.com/pod-product-compliance
Lightning Source LLC
Chambersburg PA
CBHW020910180626
46816CB00007BA/2338